Mrs. Pargeter's Plot

G·K
Hall
&Cº.

Also by Simon Brett
in Large Print:

Singled Out
Dead Romantic
Mrs. Presumed Dead
Mrs. Pargeter's Pound of Flesh
Cast, in Order of Disappearence
Star Trap
An Amateur Corpse
Not Dead, Only Resting
Dead Giveaway
What Bloody Man Is That?

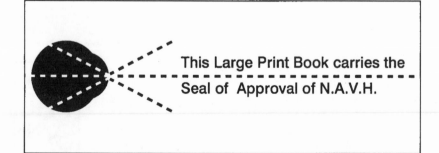

Mrs. Pargeter's Plot

A
MRS. PARGETER MYSTERY

Simon Brett

G.K. Hall & Co. • Thorndike, Maine

Published in 1998 by arrangement with Scribner, an imprint of Simon & Schuster, Inc.

G.K. Hall Large Print Mysteries.

The text of this Large Print edition is unabridged.
Other aspects of the book may vary from the original edition.

Set in 16 pt. Plantin.

Printed in the United States on permanent paper.

Library of Congress Cataloging in Publication Data

Brett, Simon.
    Mrs. Pargeter's plot : a Mrs. Pargeter mystery / Simon Brett.
      p.   cm.
    ISBN 0-7838-0172-6 (lg. print : hc : alk. paper)
    1. Pargeter, Mrs. (Fictitious character) — Fiction. 2. Women detectives — England — London — Fiction. 3. London (England) — Fiction. I. Title.
    [PR6052.R4296M374   1998b]
    823'.914—dc21   98-3644

To Beth Porter,
WHO HAD FAITH

Chapter One

'And this, Gary, is where I'll be living,' said Mrs Pargeter, as the limousine came to a halt by the gate.

'Very nice position.' The young chauffeur tipped his cap back and looked appreciatively up at the four-acre plot. It was still only a field, sloping indulgently down towards them. In a central position — surrounded by cement mixers, diggers and strapped piles of bricks — the foundations of a substantial dwelling were outlined by wooden posts and trenches. When it was completed, the house would command magnificent views over the valley below. Its outlook would be green, pastoral, with artlessly scattered clumps of trees in the folds of hills, quintessentially English.

'Never really seen you as a country person, Mrs Pargeter,' Gary went on.

'Don't know till you try, do you? That's true of everything.' The plump white-haired widow chuckled. 'Might be just the thing for my declining years — little old lady devoting her life to breeding roses and bottling chutney.'

'Can't see it.'

'Well, no, nor can I — not instinctively, like. But you never know.' The lids wrinkled round

Mrs Pargeter's violet-blue eyes as she tried to make the effort of imagination. Not achieving instant results, and not too worried by the lack of them, she moved cheerily on. 'It's only just over an hour from London, anyway. I can always escape when the birdsong and pure country air become too oppressive. Get back to my natural environment — where I can hear the birds cough, eh?'

"Suppose so, yes. I like the country,' said Gary, 'that's why Denise and me've moved out — but I reckon it might be a bit quiet for you, after the life you've led.'

Mrs Pargeter was imperturbable, as she smoothed down the bright silk skirt over her substantial thighs. 'It'll be fine. Anyway, it makes sense — economically. I've never wanted any of my money just to lie idle.' A little blush. 'And it makes sense sentimentally, too.' She responded to Gary's quizzical look. 'My husband bought the plot years ago. One of his pipe dreams, this was. Always planned that we'd build a house here for our retirement, but . . . it was not to be.'

The chauffeur nodded soberly. 'He was a saint, your husband, Mrs Pargeter.'

She indulged herself in a moment of dewy-eyed retrospection. 'Oh yes. Yes, he was.'

'Mind you, can't see him having found much to do in the country either.'

'There was a side of Mr Pargeter you never saw,' Mrs Pargeter reproved. 'A quieter, less flamboyant side. A side that would really have responded to country life and country pursuits.'

Gary chuckled. 'Huntin', shootin' and fishin', eh? Well, I can believe he might have enjoyed the shootin' bit, but . . .' In the rear-view mirror he caught the glacial violet-blue stare from his employer's eyes, and the words dried up.

Further embarrassment was fortunately prevented by the approach from the opposite direction of a mud-spattered green Range Rover. 'Ah, this'll be Concrete,' said Mrs Pargeter.

The Range Rover stopped almost bumper to bumper with the limousine, and a burly man in a checked shirt got out. He had thinning ginger curls and skin the colour of the bricks that were his stock-in-trade. He came forward with hand outstretched to greet Mrs Pargeter as she emerged from the limousine.

'Bloody marvellous to see you, Mrs P. How've you been?'

'Great, thank you, Concrete. Don't think you know Gary . . .'

The chauffeur, also by now out of the car, shook the builder's hand heartily. 'Never actually met, have we, Concrete . . . but I've heard a lot about you.'

'Nothing bad, I hope?'

'No, no. Good news all round. Everyone who worked for Mr Pargeter said Concrete Jacket was a real craftsman.'

'Oh.' The builder shrugged modestly. 'Well . . . always did my best.'

'People still talk about that tunnel you built under the Nat West bank in Chelmsford. And the safe deposit box you fixed into the side of Chelsea Barracks.'

The builder's face turned a deeper brick-red. 'Yeah, I was quite pleased with those, and all.'

'Best builder around, I heard.'

Concrete Jacket shrugged again. In spite of his embarrassment, he was enjoying this.

Mrs Pargeter's next words, however, cut him down to size. 'Best builder around — when you *are* around, yes.' Concrete looked aggrieved as she explained to Gary: 'Trouble with most builders — they're always away doing other jobs. With Concrete, though, he was always being *put* away after doing other jobs.'

'Did have a run of bad luck,' the builder conceded.

'Bad luck? You were in and out of prison like Lord Longford.'

'Well, yes, it was difficult. After your husband died, I got in with some bad company and —'

'It meant all the jobs you started kept having two- or three-year interruptions in the middle of them.'

'All right, I know. But that's all changed now. Totally different. I tell you, now I've started on this house for you, Mrs Pargeter, nothing — nothing on earth — is going to interrupt it till the job's good and finished.'

'I hope you're right,' she said darkly.

'Trust me.'

They paced through the relief map formed by the foundations. Concrete's steel-toed boots splashed unconcerned, while Mrs Pargeter's high heels and Gary's shiny black shoes negotiated the mud more circumspectly. As she looked around, Mrs Pargeter felt a little bubble of excitement at the thought of the house that would rise from these footings. It would be her dream home, her bolt-hole, a place that really expressed her personality. 'So, Concrete, I just walk out of the sitting room *here* into the dining room *here* for an elegant dinner . . .'

'Exactly.' The builder was all smiles now he was back in her good books. 'Not forgetting to pick up a nice bottle of plonk from the wine cellar.'

'There's a wine cellar?'

'You bet.' He pointed to a square opening in the ground which was covered over by a couple of planks. 'Your husband always used to say every house should have places where you can hide stuff.'

Mrs Pargeter smiled ingenuously. 'Did he? I wonder what on earth he meant . . .'

Concrete Jacket went on, 'And I can do the parquet flooring lovely so's nobody'd ever know the entrance was there.'

Still looking innocent, she asked, 'What would be the point of that, Concrete?' She moved forward, as if to lift up the covering. 'Now I'd really like to see how —'

Concrete tried to intercept her. 'Oh, I wouldn't look under there if —'

But he was too late. Mrs Pargeter had shifted the planks aside and was looking down into the void. 'So this is going to be . . . ?'

But something she saw in the embryo wine cellar caused her words to evaporate into silence.

The builder and the chauffeur moved quickly forward and they too looked down.

'Oh, my God,' Gary breathed softly.

In a pool of water that had gathered at the bottom of the bricked-in space lay a man's body. His hands had been tied behind him and in the nape of his neck was the discoloured puncture of a gunshot wound.

'Oh, my good Gawd,' said Concrete Jacket. 'I never knew I was going to find that here.'

Mrs Pargeter looked at him, and the builder's eyes shifted away from her piercing gaze. She was about to speak, but was distracted by the sound of approaching sirens. They all looked down the hill to where two police cars were screeching to a halt beside the limousine and the Range Rover.

'Well,' said Gary, picking up on Concrete's last words. 'It looks as if someone else knew you were.'

Chapter Two

The limousine drew up on a double yellow line outside a betting shop in South London. 'I'll come in with you,' said Gary, as he helped Mrs Pargeter out of the back.

'Sure. Car be all right here, will it? Don't want to waste all your profits in parking tickets, do you, Gary?'

'Be fine.' The chauffeur reached into the back door's side pocket, extracted two items and placed them on the shelf under the rear window. They were a copy of the current *Police Gazette* and a Metropolitan Police Commissioner's cap.

Mrs Pargeter grinned and led the way into the betting shop.

It was mid-afternoon and the assembled punters perched in excitement, or lounged in lethargy, on round-topped stools. She was reminded of Dr Johnson's description of a second marriage as the triumph of hope over experience. The wall-speakers crackled with the latest betting; on coloured monitors horses milled around starting stalls; the air was heavy with cigarette smoke and disappointment. The litter of crumpled and torn betting slips on the floor bore witness to the continuing and inexorable rise in the bookmakers' profits.

Mrs Pargeter's high heels picked their way daintily through the debris. Gary's neat grey uniform and peaked cap attracted more attention than her ample figure in its bright silk dress. In spite of her handsome appearance and colourful taste in clothes, Mrs Pargeter rarely looked out of place in any environment.

She moved across to the cork board on which one of the day's racing pages was pinned. She looked at the listings and checked her watch. Then she drew a fifty-pound note and a five-pound note out of her pocket, and pressed the fifty into Gary's hand.

'Prior Convictions in the three-thirty at Haydock.' He nodded. She handed across the fiver. 'And pay the tax.'

'Then shall I come to his office?'

A shake of the head. 'Wait down here.'

As Gary went to the Bet Here window, Mrs Pargeter moved across to the Pay Out. 'Looking for Mr Mason,' she said.

The thickly bespectacled girl behind the glass jerked her head towards a door marked: Private — Staff Only. 'Second floor,' she mumbled.

'Thank you.'

The narrow stairs were rendered narrower by boxes piled along their sides. Must be a real fire hazard, Mrs Pargeter thought, as she puffed upwards. The doors on the first landing bore names of travel agents, though the dust on their padlocks and the spillage of junk mail outside suggested potential clients would be well advised to look elsewhere for their dream holidays.

There was only one door on the second landing. Some long time ago it had been painted grey, and the newly applied adhesive gold lettering merely emphasized its shabbiness: MASON DE VERE DETECTIVE AGENCY.

Mrs Pargeter paused for a moment to gather her breath, then reached a hand up to the bellpush at the side of the door. But the sight of loose wire-ends spilling out of it changed her mind and she knocked instead. Receiving no reply, she pushed the door open.

The first thing she was aware of was a Welsh voice, taut with affront. '. . . and so I spend the whole weekend tidying up the garden — and it's all stuff he just left there, kept saying he'd get round to clearing it up but never did. "Oh, it's a big job, Bronwen," he was always saying, "take time that will, have to wait till I can get a week's leave." And it takes me just one weekend to clear the lot — and all the time I'm sweating away, knee-deep in garbage, I know that the bastard's sitting in some luxury hotel the other side of the world with that brainless teenager . . .'

While this diatribe continued to pour out like molten lava, Mrs Pargeter took in her surroundings. The outer office was cluttered by old files bulging with yellowed documents, piles of newspapers, telephone books and other impedimenta. The predominant colours were buff, brown and institutional green. If she hadn't known these to be new offices, she would have assumed that the

Mason De Vere Detective Agency had worked out of the premises for decades. Clearly everything — the furniture as well — had just been lifted up bodily from the old office and dumped here. Its dust may have been temporarily disturbed by the upheaval, but had by now had time to resettle exactly where it had lain in its previous environment.

The only object that looked new was a gleaming wall-planner for the current year. It was pinned proudly behind Bronwen's desk, with a little plastic container of different-coloured stickers attached to the bottom. Along the top of the chart the words MASON DE VERE DETECTIVE AGENCY had been picked out in the same adhesive gold as on the outer door. Beneath this, in contrasting silver, were the words, CURRENT COMMITMENTS. A line of coloured stickers ran down the side under the optimistic title 'Legend', but no words were offered to explain their significance. And, though it was already summer, in the virgin white daily rectangles of the year-planner there were no stickers of any colour.

Mrs Pargeter looked across at Bronwen, who was still monologuizing into the telephone. Mid-thirties, she was attractive in a dark wiry way, though her lips were tight in a perpetual grimace of annoyance. Eventually Mrs Pargeter managed to make eye contact with the girl, who seemed unfazed by and uninterested in her visitor. 'Mr Mason?' Mrs Pargeter mouthed, for some reason inhibited from intruding too forcefully into the

16

flow of Welsh vituperation.

Without drawing breath, Bronwen jerked her head towards a door. '. . . and all the time I'm thinking — only reason I have to do this is so that we can get a better price for the house — which I wouldn't have to be selling but for the way he's behaved — and then he'll simply have to pay me less in my settlement. My God, they always said there was one law for the men and one for the women. All you have to do is get born with a tassel and —'

Mrs Pargeter passed through into the inner office and the door shut off further righteous fury.

The lugubrious, horse-faced man in the wooden swivel chair looked up from what he was reading. It was a magazine, and the only dust-free item in the room. Clearly the man's desk, with its pile of papers, files, encrusted coffee cups and fluff, had also been moved intact from its previous home with all the care for exact repositioning that would attend an avant garde sculpture in the Tate Gallery.

'Mrs Pargeter,' he intoned dolefully, unwinding his surprising height as he rose from the chair. 'Mrs Pargeter! How wonderful to see you!'

'Great to see you too, Truffler.' She gave his outstretched hand a little squeeze. 'See you've got De Vere back.'

'What?'

She nodded her head towards the outer office. 'Sorry. Always think of her as De Vere. Other half of the agency.'

'There isn't another half of the agency. I just put the "De Vere" in to make it sound more impressive.'

'I know that. Still always think of Bronwen as De Vere, though.'

'Well, she's not a partner — only my secretary,' said Truffler with slightly dented professional pride. 'Handles the telephone.'

'And how! Handles it like a shearer handles a sheep.' Mrs Pargeter grinned. 'Taking on staff again, eh? This mean the recession's bottoming out for you, does it?'

'Wouldn't say that.' Truffler's normally mournful tone took on a note of deeper pessimism. 'Business still very shaky, I'm afraid. No, I got Bronwen back, because . . . well, she'd got problems — you know, divorce and . . .'

'This must be the longest divorce in history. I mean, last time she was working for you, you said she was in the middle of a very sticky divorce.'

'Yes. This is another divorce.'

'Oh. You mean she went off and remarried?'

'Mm. And now she's redivorcing.'

For the second time that afternoon Mrs Pargeter was reminded of Dr Johnson's words about the triumph of hope over experience. 'She must be a glutton for punishment.'

'If that's what Bronwen is, what does it make the men who keep marrying her?' asked Truffler gloomily. 'Anyway, what can I do for you, Mrs Pargeter? Anything, anything at all.'

'I'm not interrupting, am I? Should you be

18

concentrating on your reading? Is it something important?'

'No, it's only the Lag Mag.'

Her violet-blue eyes peered at him curiously for an explanation.

' "Lag Mag" — that's what it gets nicknamed. Really called *Inside Out.*'

'And it's a kind of specialist magazine, is it?'

'You could say that.' He let out a mournful chuckle. 'Yes, it's for specialists who might be interested in . . . people's movements.'

'People's movements?' she echoed, perplexed. 'You're not talking about aerobics, are you?'

'No, no. I'm talking about who's going in, who's coming out . . .'

From her expression, this was clearly insufficient information, so Truffler Mason elaborated. '. . . who's being transferred . . . you know, from High Security to Category B . . . Cat. C to an Open Prison . . . who's got time off for good behaviour . . . all that kind of stuff.'

Mrs Pargeter's mouth hardened into a line of prim disapproval. 'Prisoners, you mean? I didn't think you had anything to do with that kind of person now, Truffler.'

'I don't, I don't. Not professionally. I don't work with them. But I still need this kind of information. I do a lot of Missing Persons work, you know.'

'Are you telling me that you're one of the so-called "specialists" for whom this magazine is intended?' Her tone had not lost its tartness.

19

'In a way, yes.'

'So are most of these "specialists" private detectives?'

'No, most of them are . . . I don't know . . . girlfriends who want a bit of warning to get the new lover out before the old man comes back . . . villains who've got scores to settle . . . poor bastards who've got scores to be settled against them . . . geezers who know where the stash is buried . . . grasses who aren't sure whether their change of identity has worked . . . that kind of stuff.'

'I don't see that you fit into any of those categories, Truffler.'

He looked aggrieved, as hangdog as a Labrador wrongly accused of eating the Sunday joint. 'But I need to know that kind of info, Mrs P. Listen, someone hires me to work out who's nicked their jewellery what the police've had no luck finding . . . OK, I check out the MO, and know that there's only three villains in the country works that way . . . I check through *here* . . .' He tapped the magazine on his desk for emphasis. Puffs of dust rose like a Red Indian signal telling that the US Cavalry was nearing the ravine where they'd be ripe for ambush. '. . . and I find out that two of the geezers who fit the frame were, on the night of the fifteenth, in Strangeways and Parkhurst respectively. So I know who my man is, don't I?'

'Yes, I see what you mean.' Mrs Pargeter, who always owned up straight away when she found herself in the wrong, looked properly contrite. 'Sorry. Shouldn't have distrusted you, Truffler.'

He shrugged forgiveness. 'Nah. Think nothing of it. I appreciate the fact you care enough for it to upset you. But don't you have no worries on that score. I been on the right side of the law since the moment that your husband . . . er . . .' He wove his long fingers together in embarrassment as he tried to shape the word.

'Died?' Mrs Pargeter supplied easily.

'Yes.' Relieved to move off the subject, he once again tapped his copy of *Inside Out* on the desk, beaming up another warlike message to the Shoshoni. 'And this is an invaluable means of keeping tabs on former colleagues . . . you know, seeing where they are, when they'll be back in circulation again. Dead useful when it comes to doing my Christmas card list.'

'All right, all right.' Mrs Pargeter grinned. 'I think you've convinced me that the magazine's an essential tool of your trade.'

'Not just that,' Truffler persisted. 'It's also a very useful Early Warning System.'

'Oh?'

He nodded grimly. 'Oh yes. For instance, this very week, I discover, Fossilface O'Donahue will be out.'

'Fossilface O'Donahue?' she echoed.

Truffler Mason found the relevant page in his copy of *Inside Out*, and held it open across the desk to Mrs Pargeter. The photograph which confronted her showed the aptness of its subject's nickname. The face did indeed look like a relic from an age before the invention of the wheel, or of human sensitivity, or of compassion. Though the picture was in black and white, she got the feeling it wouldn't have looked very different in colour. The face was a slab of grey, with that pumicestone surface of the heavy smoker. The eyes, which can normally be relied on to lend animation to a face, were dull, dark pebbles, lurking resentfully deep in two parallel crevices. Mrs Pargeter looked up at Truffler. 'Should I know him?'

'No, I don't think you should. Be a lot better all round if you never do know him. Mean, vengeful bastard, without a glimmer of a sense of humour. Slippery, too — always used to come out of hiding to do a job, then apparently disappear off the face of the earth. Bad news all round, I'd say.' He paused, choosing his words with circumspection. 'Mind you, your husband did know him, and he and Fossilface didn't always see eye to eye on everything, so I'm going to be keeping a close watch on the geezer's . . . what shall I call it . . . re-entry into society?'

'You think there might be danger from this . . . Fossilface? Danger for me?'

'No, there won't be,' Truffler reassured her. 'Not now I know he's coming out. You'll be as safe as houses. See — I told you *Inside Out* was useful. He can settle any other scores he wants to — that I don't care about — but Fossilface O'Donahue is not going to come near you, Mrs P.'

It was not the first time she had had cause to

be grateful for the comprehensive network of care the late Mr Pargeter had organized for his survivor. She reached across the desk and placed her hand on Truffler Mason's huge knuckles. 'Bless you. I do appreciate the way you look after me, you know.'

'Think nothing of it. Entirely my pleasure. And what else can I do for you now, eh? I'm sure you haven't just turned up to admire the colour of my wallpaper.' No, thought Mrs Pargeter, *nobody* could possibly have turned up to admire the colour of that wallpaper. 'So what is it, Mrs P.? Come on, you tell Truffler.'

'Well,' she began. 'Well, I don't want to take up your time if you've got other things on your desk that you should be —'

With one gesture of his long sports-jacketed forearm, Truffler Mason swept everything off the dusty wooden surface. It clattered to the floor, with an effect that must have jammed the Red Indian signals' switchboard.

'Nothing else on my desk,' he announced with what, on a less permanently despondent face, would have been a grin.

Chapter Three

'I swear he didn't know the body was there,' Mrs Pargeter concluded, after describing the unpleasant discovery she'd made in what might one day become her wine cellar — assuming that she ever had a builder on site to complete it.

'But didn't Concrete say anything to let him off the hook?' asked Truffler. 'He must've at least offered an alibi. It's not as if he doesn't know the score.'

'No, that was strange. He hardly said a word when the police come. Went all quiet — almost like he was afraid of something.'

The private detective rubbed his long chin thoughtfully, as she went on, 'Anyway, I'm sure that this killing's not Concrete Jacket's style. If he was going to do away with someone — and I somehow can't imagine he ever would — but *if* he did, he'd go for a method a bit more subtle than a bullet in the back of the neck. And he'd get rid of the body somewhere way off his own patch. He knows all the rules about not fouling your own footpath.'

'He wouldn't do it, anyway, Mrs P. — not murder. Wouldn't do anything seriously wonky these days. Concrete's been pretty well straight ever since your husband, er . . .' Truffler's words petered out in another apologetic little cough.

Mrs Pargeter gracefully skirted round the potential embarrassment by ignoring it. 'You're right. He might rip off the odd sub-contractor, overcharge a client or play fast and loose with his VAT returns, but that's normal business practice in the building trade. He'd never get involved in murder, though. No, somebody's framed him good and proper. They knew he was going to be at the site at that time and tipped off the police. Rozzers'd got all the details — arrested him straight away, no arguments. And, of course, it doesn't help that Concrete's got form.'

Truffler's reaction was instinctive. 'Who hasn't?'

The violet-blue surface of Mrs Pargeter's eyes frosted over. 'I wouldn't know.'

Truffler hastened to cover up his *faux pas*. 'No. No, of course you wouldn't.' A fond and misty expression spread down his long face. 'Ah, when I think back to all those times working with your husband . . . He was a prince among men, Mrs Pargeter, a real prince.'

Mrs Pargeter, finding the emotion contagious, nodded.

'Taught me the lot. I couldn't be doing what I'm doing now without Mr Pargeter, you know. He taught me how to apply the talents I had to crime.' He corrected himself. 'The *solution* of crime, that is. No, he was a diamond.' But this was no time for nostalgia. Truffler straightened up in his chair. 'Police didn't happen to let drop who the stiff was, did they?'

'No. I tried to get it out of them, but they went all very strait-laced Mr Plod on me. "We are conducting our enquiries in our own way, thank you very much, Madam, and we're not in the habit of giving members of the public privileged information." No sense of humour, the police, never did have.'

'Leave it with me,' said Truffler. 'I'll get the full history on the dead geezer — right down to his collar size and his favourite flavour of crisps. And don't you worry about a thing, Mrs P. We'll get Concrete off the hook, no problem.'

'I hope so,' said Mrs Pargeter, rising to leave. 'Otherwise I'm never going to get my house finished.'

'You, er . . . wouldn't think of using another builder?'

She looked affronted. 'No, Truffler. I do have my standards of loyalty, you know.'

'Yes, of course you do. Sorry.' Truffler once again uncoiled himself from his chair to see her to the door. 'Oh, one point. Where do I contact you? You renting a place at the moment or what?'

'I'm at Greene's Hotel for the foreseeable.'

'Hedgeclipper Clinton's place?'

'That's right.'

'I hope he's looking after you properly.'

'I'm being spoilt rotten.'

'Great. You deserve it.'

As soon as the door opened, they were aware of the continuing Welsh saga of masculine perfidy. '. . . and then, to cap it all, I get home yesterday and there's a message on the answerphone from him, asking if I could take two of his suits to the dry cleaners. "Don't worry, I'll pick them up and pay for them when I get back from Mauritius," he says. The bloody nerve! Well, I took them somewhere, you'd better believe it — but it wasn't the dry cleaners. No, I put them in a couple of half-empty bags of organic fertilizer and took them down the municipal tip with all the rubbish I cleared from the back garden. Let him pick them up from there when he gets "back from Mauritius". Honestly, you'd never believe that this was the man who . . .'

Bronwen was completely oblivious of their presence. Truffler gave an apologetic shrug as he saw his guest through the outer door.

'Does she ever do any work?' asked Mrs Pargeter curiously.

The detective looked uncomfortable. 'Well, I'm sure she will get back to working properly soon. She's a bit upset at the moment, what with the divorce and that, so, you know, I don't want to press it.'

Mrs Pargeter shook her head. 'You're too soft. Remember, you're running a business here, Truffler, and the recession's still not completely bottomed out.'

He hung his head sheepishly. 'Nah, you're right.' Although Bronwen was far too preoccupied with her own grievances to be listening, he lowered his voice. 'Thing is with her, apart from anything else, we haven't got any of the right work going, so there's not that much she could be doing at the moment. When we get one of her speciality cases, she'll be on to it like a terrier, work her little socks off, no one can touch her.'

'What are her speciality cases?'

'Matrimonial.'

'Ah, that would figure.'

'Worth her weight in gold, Bronwen is, when we've got some poor little wife suspects her husband's doing naughties. Do you know, she once staked out a motel for a whole month, twenty-four hours a day, and produced this great dossier of all the times the man in question went in and out. Every single detail, lovely piece of work it was.'

'So then she presented the wife with evidence of adultery, did she?'

Truffler coloured. 'Well, no. Trouble is, the wife hadn't told her the husband actually *worked* at the motel as a chef, but I merely mention it to show how hard-working Bronwen can be when she's got the right sort of case.'

'Fine,' said Mrs Pargeter. 'You've convinced me. Cheerio, Truffler. Be in touch.'

'. . . and if I could have threaded barbed wire into his boxer shorts, I would've!' were the last Welsh words she heard as the door closed behind her.

Downstairs Gary was perched on a stool watching the horses getting into the stalls for 4.00 at Lingfield. Rising to his feet as Mrs Pargeter approached, he reached into his pocket and handed her a bundle of fifty-pound notes.

'Had you heard something from the yard about that horse Prior Convictions?'

'No,' Mrs Pargeter replied with a little smile. 'Just liked the name.'

Chapter Four

The mid-morning sun fell on the windows of Greene's Hotel, but the curtains of Mrs Pargeter's suite were far too opulent to allow any of it in. She lay in the bedroom, under the mound of her duvet, exhaling evenly with a sound that was just the gracious side of a snore.

The suite was decorated with gratuitous antiques to appeal to the American guests who formed the backbone of Hedgeclipper Clinton's clientele. In heavy frames on the wall hung assemblages of fruit and dead poultry, interspersed with eighteenth-century portraits of unmemorable people's even less memorable relatives. The carpet and curtains were deep, as was the shine on the dark oak furniture and the brass light fittings.

Mrs Pargeter had made no attempt to impose her own style on the rooms. All her furniture was in store. The stay at Greene's Hotel had been originally intended as a short one, but comfort and convenience had kept her longer. She had then decided that she might as well stay until her house was completed, and had not yet reassessed the situation since recent events had moved that horizon yet nearer to infinity.

The only personal touch in the suite was a

silver-framed photograph on Mrs Pargeter's bed-side table. It was a studio portrait of a highly respectable-looking gentleman in a pinstriped suit.

The telephone — in the tasteful antique style which would have been the automatic selection of any Regency gentleman, had telephones been available in those times — rang, summoning Mrs Pargeter from a blissful dream of sunlight and strawberries. As she reached blearily towards the bedside table, her eye caught the photograph. 'Morning, love,' she said to the late Mr Pargeter.

She picked up the receiver. 'Hello?'

'Mrs Pargeter,' said the French-polished tones of the hotel's manager.

'Morning, Hedgeclipper.'

This was greeted by a discreet admonitory cough. 'I believe I did request you not to use that name within the purlieus of the hotel, Mrs Pargeter.'

'Oh yes, forgive me. Half asleep.'

'Well, I'm very sorry to have been the cause of the interruption of your slumbers, but there's a gentleman down here in the foyer who wishes to see you as a matter of some urgency.'

'That sounds exciting. Who is he?'

'His name is Mr Nigel Merriman.'

'Doesn't ring a bell. Should I know him?'

The poshness of Hedgeclipper Clinton's accent slipped instantly away, to reveal the original Bermondsey beneath. 'He's only Concrete Jacket's bloomin' solicitor, isn't he?'

Once she was dressed, Mrs Pargeter would have gone straight downstairs to breakfast and Nigel Merriman had she not found something rather unusual in the sitting room of her suite.

It was a monkey.

She thought she'd heard some rather strange noises while she was dressing, but put them down to a quirk of the hotel's air conditioning or some extravagance of one of the other guests. (It took only a short stay in Greene's Hotel for the average person to become extremely broad-minded about the behaviour of other guests, and of course, when it came to broad-mindedness, Mrs Pargeter had a considerable head start over the average person.)

But when she went through to the sitting room, the noises — pitched somewhere between a chatter and a whimper — were immediately explained.

It was a nice enough little monkey, if you happen to like monkeys (which Mrs Pargeter decidedly didn't). It was about the size of a rat (and to her mind the similarities didn't stop there) with brownish fur and a doom-laden little old man's face. Had Mrs Pargeter had any interest in the subject, she might have recognized from its size and colouring, or from the fact that its hind limbs were 25 per cent longer than its forelimbs, that she was looking at a South American marmoset, a member of the *Callitrichidae* family, from the suborder *Anthropoidea* of the Primate order.

However, nothing could have interested her less, so she neither knew nor cared.

Around the creature's neck was a padded crimson velvet collar, to which had been attached a silver chain. The loop at the end of the chain had been slipped round the leg of a heavy oak dresser. Scratches on the wood and surrounding carpet suggested that the monkey had tried to break free, but without success.

Its reaction to Mrs Pargeter's entrance was one of excitement rather than fear. Here, it seemed to feel, was not a threat, but a potential saviour — or even playmate. This suggested that the animal was accustomed to human society, and had possibly been someone's pet.

The monkey rose up on its hind legs — clearly a party trick for Mrs Pargeter's benefit — and chattered in an almost human manner. One thin-fingered hand tugged pitifully at its chain, while the dark eyes looked up appealingly into hers. 'Set me free,' it seemed to be saying. 'Set me free.'

'In your dreams, sweetheart,' said Mrs Pargeter, as she left the room.

Hedgeclipper Clinton was by Reception when she emerged from the lift into the foyer. He gave her a smile of unctuous sincerity.

'There's a monkey in my room. Could you deal with it, please?' said Mrs Pargeter as she passed through into the dining room.

The Greene's Hotel 'Full English Breakfast'

was extremely full. No refinement of bacon, egg, sausage, tomato, grilled mushroom, fried bread, sauté potato, kidney or black pudding was omitted from the piled plate into which Mrs Pargeter tucked. Some mornings, in a momentary pang of righteousness, she asked the waitress not to include the fried bread, but this morning was not one of them. She had the tingling feeling of beginning to be involved in an investigation, and needed to keep her strength up.

Opposite her in the sumptuous setting of the *fin de siècle* dining room, sat a thin-faced, earnest-looking man in his thirties. He wore an anonymously smart charcoal suit and sober tie. His right hand, slightly nervous on the crisp linen, toyed with the handle of his coffee cup.

'Sure you won't have anything else, Mr Merriman?' asked Mrs Pargeter, after a delicious mouthful of sausage, egg and sauté potato.

'No, really, thank you,' Nigel Merriman replied. 'I breakfasted earlier.'

Mrs Pargeter loaded her fork with another consignment of bacon, egg, tomato and fried bread. 'Well, you won't mind me, I hope?'

'Of course not.'

She gestured permission with her heaped fork. 'You talk while I eat. Seems a fair division of labour.'

'Yes.' He allowed himself a prim silence while he collected his thoughts and Mrs Pargeter munched contentedly. 'What I'm really after . . . is anything you might know that could help in

Mr Jacket's defence.'

The fullness of Mrs Pargeter's mouth excluded all responses other than an 'Mm.'

'At the moment I'm afraid my client's situation does look rather grim.'

The mouth was by now decorously empty. 'Oh? You mean he actually had some connection with the dead man?'

'I'm afraid so.'

Mrs Pargeter wiped the side of her mouth with a napkin. 'Who was the stiff then?'

Nigel Merriman could not suppress a slight wince at the colloquialism before replying, 'A bricklayer and part-time villain called Willie Cass. Worked with Mr Jacket till relatively recently, but was dismissed when found to be selling on bricks and other materials his employer had paid for.'

She nodded. 'If anyone was going to be ripping off the clients, the boss thought it should be him rather than one of his staff, eh?'

'Exactly.'

'So has this just happened? I mean, they've only recently fallen out, have they?'

'No, we're talking a year ago. Unfortunately, though, Willie Cass has spent the last month shooting his mouth off round a lot of South London pubs, saying how he'd got some dirt on Concrete Jacket — Mr Jacket is nicknamed —'

'I know.'

'Anyway, Willie Cass was saying that Concrete would have to pay a great deal for his silence.'

'Blackmail,' said Mrs Pargeter, stacking another pensive forkful.

'Mm.' The solicitor cleared his throat, about to negotiate something unpalatable. 'There is a further regrettable circumstance . . . in that the gun used to kill Willie Cass is owned by Mr Jacket.'

'Oh.'

'Illegally, I'm afraid.'

'Ah.'

'All of which, together with his previous record, makes things look a little uncomfortable for my client.'

'I can see that.'

'Particularly since the client in question seems unwilling to provide any information himself that might help his cause.'

'I heard. Odd, that, isn't it? You'd have thought it would be a point of honour for Concrete to at least come up with an alibi.'

The solicitor shrugged. 'Well, he won't. There are any number of things he could say that might help get him off the hook . . . and he's not saying any of them.'

'You think someone's putting the frighteners on him? Do you think he's protecting someone?'

'Your guess is as good as mine, Mrs Pargeter. I can't get at his reasons. All I know is that he seems determined to make things as easy as possible for the police prosecutors.'

Mrs Pargeter looked puzzled as she pushed her empty plate away and began absent-mindedly to

smother a piece of toast with butter and marmalade.

Nigel Merriman opened his hands out in appeal. 'So anything you can think of, Mrs Pargeter
. . . anything you heard Mr Jacket say, anything
you remember that happened down at the site
. . . please let me know before you tell anyone
else.'

Mrs Pargeter looked affronted. 'Who else do
you think I might tell?'

'The police?'

She chuckled. 'You clearly don't know me, Mr
Merriman.'

'No.' He paused, then spoke as if confiding
something rather special. 'Only by reputation.'

'Oh?'

The solicitor rationed himself a thin smile.
'Which reputation makes me absolutely certain I
want you on my side in trying to clear my client.'

Mrs Pargeter nodded in acknowledgement of
the compliment. 'Unusual for someone in your
profession to be so concerned, Mr Merriman.
There aren't that many solicitors who want to get
involved with acknowledged villains — even villains who've been going straight for as long as
Concrete has.'

'What you say is true. Perhaps my different
attitude derives from the somewhat unusual circumstances by which I came into my chosen profession.' In response to her quizzical look, Nigel
Merriman elaborated. 'I was lucky enough to be
put through Law College, and supported through

my articles . . . by a benefactor.' Another small smile. 'His name was Mr Pargeter.'

'Really?' Mrs Pargeter nodded her understanding and beamed. Her late husband had shown great altruism in saving a lot of young people from dead-end lives by sponsoring their training. The list had included accountants, solicitors, barristers, doctors and journalists. And in each case the late Mr Pargeter's altruism had continued to the extent of finding gainful employment for his protégés once they had qualified. She smiled at Nigel Merriman. 'He always used to say it was very useful to have a solicitor on your side.'

A look of appropriate reverence came into the young man's face. 'He was a great philanthropist, your husband, Mrs Pargeter.'

'Oh yes,' the widow agreed fondly. 'Yes, he was.'

Chapter Five

Clearly, dealing with the monkey was not proving easy. Hedgeclipper Clinton was too preoccupied by his task to be aware of Mrs Pargeter's return to her suite. She stood in the doorway and watched the scene with considerable relish.

The hotel manager had freed the marmoset's chain from its anchorage to the dresser, but the animal had evidently escaped and showed no relish for recapture. It was now perched on the pelmet, high above the tall windows, chattering at its pursuer with uninhibited amusement. In one hand the creature held a banana, an attempted bait that it must have snatched and got away with. Between chattering noises, the marmoset detached lumps of the fruit and swirled them around in its saliva, before hurling them towards the hotel manager. That its aim was unerring could be seen from the splodges on Hedgeclipper Clinton's black tailcoat.

The general chaos of the room — overturned chairs, paintings askew, torn curtains and banana-smeared surfaces — suggested the chase had been lively and vigorous. And that the monkey was very definitely in control of the situation.

The volume of fruit splattered around the room showed Hedgeclipper Clinton must have come in with a considerable supply of bananas, but he was now running out. He held up the last one, its skin peeled back to show the tempting white flesh, imploringly towards the marmoset, while he murmured in seductive tones, 'Come on, Erasmus. Come on, Erasmus, there's a good boy . . .'

'Why on earth "Erasmus"?' asked Mrs Pargeter from the doorway.

'Oh, I didn't hear you come in.' He turned to look at her. 'I had an uncle who had a pet monkey called Erasmus. Thereafter, I'm afraid, all monkeys have been Erasmus so far as I'm concerned.'

Hedgeclipper Clinton shouldn't have taken his eyes off his quarry. The marmoset, acute to the lapse of concentration, leapt in one easy movement from pelmet to chandelier, gripped the stem with one nonchalantly prehensile foot, swung downwards to snatch the banana, and was back on the pelmet before the hotel manager had turned round again.

'Damn,' he said. Then, as another sucked blob of pulp caught him in the eye, 'Damn!'

'Good luck,' said Mrs Pargeter, as she went smiling through into the bedroom. 'I'm relying on you to sort it out, Hedgeclipper.'

Gary's limousine slid effortlessly out of the Dartford Tunnel on its way towards Essex. In the back, over glasses of chilled Chardonnay from the vehicle's bar, Mrs Pargeter brought Truffler Mason up to date on the case.

'I mean, I'm sure it was just coincidence that

I was there at the site when the police came. I'd only rung Concrete that morning and said I'd like to have a look at how the building was going. And then I'd rung Gary and he was free —'

'Always free for you, Mrs Pargeter,' the chauffeur chipped in.

'Less of that, young man,' she said sharply. 'You got your own business now.'

'I know. But when I think of everything your husband taught me, the least I can do is to —'

'If I know anything about my husband,' Mrs Pargeter continued in the same tone of reproof, 'he also taught you that there is no room in the commercial world for sentimentality. Compassion — yes. Sentimentality — no. You're running a hire-car business, young Gary — you take all the bookings you can, and see that everyone pays. Including me.'

Subdued, Gary nodded his acceptance of this. But it was an ongoing running battle between them and he'd only lost the skirmish. In time he would return to the fray with ever more devious attempts to undercharge his favourite client — or ideally not to charge her at all.

Mrs Pargeter resumed her conversation with Truffler. 'And the stuff you got on Willie Cass fits in with what Nigel Merriman told me, does it?'

A rueful nod. 'Down to the last detail. I mean, I got feelers out, I'll get some more info, but . . . The daft thing about it is how public Willie was about blackmailing Concrete. Short of buying ad-

41

vertising in the middle of *Coronation Street*, he couldn't have let more people know what he was up to.'

'Yes, there's so much evidence against Concrete, it's got to be a frame-up.'

'Certainly. Whole case is far too tidy. All neatly tied up with a bow on top.' Truffler grimaced wryly. 'Trouble is . . .'

'Hm?'

'The police *like* cases all neatly tied up with a bow on top.'

'That may be so,' she remonstrated, 'but this time surely anyone with a bit of imagination could see that —'

Truffler raised a hand politely to interrupt her. 'Er, not "anyone with a bit of imagination". I did say the police, Mrs Pargeter.'

'True.' She sighed glumly, took a swig of Chardonnay, and sank back into the limousine's plush upholstery. 'Oh well, maybe we can get some more stuff from Tammy.'

The Jackets lived outside Basildon in a large modern house on which everything had been lavished but taste. The house was full of 'features' — windows of different shapes glazed in different styles and colours, walls of exposed brick, walls draped in hessian, walls covered in flock, vinyl and panelling. Interior doors ranged from studded monastic oak to chest-high Western saloon. Artex whirled, carpets swirled, and cocktail trolleys proliferated. There was a lot of wrought-iron, gilt and onyx; coloured glass figurines decorated every surface.

For a moment Mrs Pargeter wondered whether the discordant styles simply reflected their owner's light fingers. Had Concrete knocked off one item from every job he did and combined them all in his home? Or was his house a kind of living catalogue, round which prospective clients could be conducted to select their own fittings from the wide range on display?

But both explanations seemed at odds with the pride demonstrated by Tammy Jacket as she showed her guests round the place. No, the style was *not* accidental. This was actually how the Jackets *wanted* their house to look.

There was another clue to this in Tammy's dress sense. She wore gilt leggings, and shoes encrusted with diamante. Her jumper was adorned with those random scraps of silver leather, bits of gilded chain and irrelevant tassels that denote purchase in a boutique for people with more money than taste. A spectrum of glittery eye-shadows vied for attention on the crow's feet around her lids, and the lacquered superstructure of her hair was the colour of a reproduction copper kettle. Tammy Jacket was of a piece with her environment.

But despite her brassy appearance, there was an engaging innocence about the woman. Though He had perhaps been a little parsimonious when He allocated her quota of intelligence, God had more than made up for it by lavish rations of charm. It was impossible not to warm to Tammy Jacket.

The three of them — Tammy, Truffler and Mrs Pargeter — sat on a three-piece suite, whose colours screamed at the carpet. The carpet screamed back at the suite, and both joined forces to scream at their owner's clothes.

'Cheers,' said Tammy Jacket cosily, and each of them raised a gold-patterned glass, filled with a dayglo drink on whose surface bright paper umbrellas wallowed in an archipelago of fruit.

'So you saw Willie Cass quite recently?' asked Mrs Pargeter, after a surprisingly rewarding sip from her glass.

Tammy nodded. 'Oh yes. He come round here. Month or so back. Sunday lunchtime it was. I remember 'cause it was Concrete's fifty-fifth birthday. We was giving this big party, lots of friends and that — and then Willie Cass appeared. No manners — he never did have any. I mean, what kind of person comes round to your house Sunday lunchtime when you're giving a party what he hasn't been invited to?'

'The kind of person who wants a lot of witnesses to see them turn up?' Truffler suggested.

'Oh, I never thought of that,' said Tammy.

'And how did Willie behave when he was here?' asked Mrs Pargeter.

'Dreadful. Way out of order. He was drunk, I reckon. Must've been. Kept saying he wanted money from Concrete — or else.'

'Or else what?'

'Didn't say exactly, but it wasn't a trip to Eurodisney.'

'No.' Mrs Pargeter looked thoughtful. 'I think you're right, Truffler. Sounds like a heavy set-up for a very public row. How did it end, Tammy?'

'Well, eventually we just had to turn him out. Fortunately, wasn't a problem. Lot of Concrete's, er, business associates was here, so they dealt with it.'

'But Concrete himself wasn't violent to Willie?'

'No, no, Mrs Pargeter. Concrete's not a violent man,' said Tammy Jacket with the sublime confidence of a trusting wife.

'Not violent, perhaps . . .' Mrs Pargeter probed, '. . . but he still kept a gun here? I understand the gun that killed Willie Cass has been identified as belonging to your husband.'

Chapter Six

If Mrs Pargeter had been hoping that her question would produce a reaction of guilt, she was disappointed. Tammy's shrug dismissed it as an irrelevance. 'Yeah, the gun was here, but that was from way back. Kind of thing you forget you've still got. You know, like the other day, I was in the loft and I come across a baby buggy. Got to be twenty years since we last needed that, but, you know, you don't think about things when you're not using them.'

Truffler looked sceptical. 'And you're saying that's how it was with the gun?'

There was no doubting the innocence of Tammy's reply. 'Quite honestly, it was only when the police asked, I remembered we'd still got it.'

'Except you hadn't still got it,' Mrs Pargeter pointed out.

'No. Right. Well, it'd been nicked, hadn't it?'

'But you've no idea when it was nicked?'

'Sorry, Truffler.' Tammy looked contrite. 'When the police asked, I told them where we kept it, but when we looked, it wasn't there.'

Mrs Pargeter and the detective exchanged glances. The openness of Tammy Jacket's naivety was of the kind that could give wrong signals to a suspicious policeman. Her artless statements of truth could sound like impudent defiance, and all too easily do a disservice to her husband's cause.

Mrs Pargeter cleared her throat. 'Going back to Willie Cass . . .'

'Mm?'

'He didn't say why he wanted money from Concrete? Didn't say what kind of hold he might have over your husband? Didn't give any inkling of what it was about?'

Tammy Jacket shook her head. 'No. But if it was something wonky, it must've gone back a long way, 'cause Concrete's been straight since . . . well, since after your husband died, Mrs Pargeter.' There was a pause. 'I never actually met your husband, but from all accounts —'

The paragon's widow, unequal at that moment to another tribute, moved the conversation quickly on. 'Yes, yes, he was.' She fixed her violet-blue eyes sternly on Tammy's hazel ones. 'But you're sure that since then Concrete hasn't been involved in anything he shouldn't have been?'

'No, no,' the loyal wife insisted instinctively. Then honesty prevailed. 'Well . . .'

Mrs Pargeter was immediately alert. 'What?'

'Well . . .' Tammy confessed with reluctance, 'he did sometimes do jobs for cash and forget the VAT — the VAT man's after him for that, actually — but then, I mean, that goes with the territory. He's a *builder*, after all, isn't he?'

Mrs Pargeter relaxed. 'Yes. Yes, of course.'

'And a very good builder at that,' Truffler endorsed. 'Job Concrete done on that tunnel between Spud-U-Like and the Midland Bank in Milton Keynes — magic. Wonderful feat of engineering — Brunel wouldn't've been ashamed of that one. Don't you agree, Mrs Pargeter?'

'I don't know what you're talking about, Truffler,' his employer replied frostily.

Truffler covered his uncharacteristic lapse as best he could. 'No, no, of course not.'

Tammy Jacket added to her husband's glowing testimonials. 'Concrete was even asked to do work abroad, you know, he was that good.'

'Oh yes?' The casual nature of Mrs Pargeter's response belied her alertness.

Tammy reached to a brass and onyx magazine rack beside her chair and pulled out a glossy folder, which she opened to extract an equally glossy prospectus. On the cover was a photograph of a lavish sun-drenched villa standing at the centre of a secluded beach. Deep blue sea and lighter blue sky framed the perfect setting. The builder's wife could not restrain her pride as she handed the prospectus across. 'Couple of years back he done this,' she announced.

Mrs Pargeter was properly impressed. She turned the pages to reveal more of the villa's exclusive and exotic features. The presentation of the details was very lavish and upmarket.

'Concrete designed the villa himself, and all,' said Tammy proudly.

'Very nice.'

Mrs Pargeter passed the brochure across to Truffler, who scrutinized it for a moment before asking, 'Where is it then? One of the Costas?'

'Nah. Lot more exotic than that. Brazil.'

'Blimey. Ronnie Biggs country. I didn't know Concrete was such a jet-setter.'

'Oh yes. Trouble was,' Tammy went on, drawing a glossy photograph out of the folder, 'he only done the one. They must've got local builders to do the rest.'

She handed the photograph across. It depicted the same beach, but the villa Concrete had built was now at the centre of a large development. Other identical villas in well-separated plots covered the waterfront.

'Still,' Tammy reassured herself, 'I suppose Concrete got paid all right for what he done. Mustn't grumble.'

She smiled with her customary placid good humour, and Mrs Pargeter commented, 'I can't help noticing, Tammy — I mean, given the fact that your husband's just been arrested for murder, and appears not to have an alibi or anything — you seem remarkably calm about the whole business.'

Tammy shrugged ingenuously. 'Yeah. Well, no point in worrying, is there?'

'Why not?'

'Concrete didn't do it . . .'

'No-o,' Mrs Pargeter agreed cautiously. 'We all know that, but I'm not —'

'. . . so that means he'll get off, dunnit?' the builder's wife concluded with a cheerful grin.

Mrs Pargeter and Truffler Mason exchanged

looks, wondering where Tammy Jacket had spent the last fifty years, and both wishing they could share her unshakeable belief in the efficiency of British justice.

Back at Greene's Hotel and before getting the lift, Mrs Pargeter thought she should check that her room had been cleaned of extraneous banana. The girl at Reception told her that Mr Clinton was in his office. And no, she said in some embarrassment, it wouldn't quite be convenient for him to come out at that precise moment. Would, Mrs Pargeter asked, there be any objection to her going into his office to talk to him there? The girl seemed confused by the question, but cautiously concluded that she couldn't really see any objection, no.

A tap on the office door prompted no reaction, though from inside Mrs Pargeter could hear sounds of Hedgeclipper Clinton's voice speaking softly, intimately. Was it possible that he had a lover in there? The idea seemed too incongruous to be allowed credence. She had no idea what Hedgeclipper Clinton did for a sex life, but Mrs Pargeter felt certain that he would always keep business and pleasure firmly separate. Around his hotel, the manager behaved with a ritual decorum which by comparison would have made the average Catholic archbishop at Mass look slovenly.

So she pushed the door open, and was immediately confronted by the object of Hedgeclipper Clinton's affections. On the polished oak desk in front of him, circled by fruit peel and nutshells, sat Erasmus.

The hotel manager was feeding the marmoset grapes with his bare hands, oblivious to the streaks that the creature gleefully smeared on to the black sleeves of his morning coat. And, as he proffered the fruit, Hedgeclipper Clinton murmured blissfully, 'There's a lovely boy, there's a lovely boy. Who's Daddy's lovely boy then?'

' "Daddy's"?' echoed Mrs Pargeter, as the door closed behind her. 'Are you proposing to reverse Darwin's theory, Hedgeclipper?'

The marmoset cocked a wary little old man's eye towards her, and the hotel manager turned guiltily, like a schoolboy surprised with a cigarette. 'Oh, I'm so sorry, Mrs Pargeter. You rather caught me on the hop, I'm afraid. I was just trying to rehabilitate this poor creature. I'm afraid he has been rather traumatized by his recent experiences.'

'Has he?' She looked sceptically at the monkey. It returned her gaze with defiance, then looked away. It could recognize someone who wasn't going to be seduced by its winsome charm. 'Poor little mite,' she said drily.

'They are very sensitive creatures, you know,' Hedgeclipper argued. 'Very highly strung. My uncle told me the original Erasmus had a maid whose only job was to look after him twenty-four hours a day.'

Mrs Pargeter looked at the hotel manager curiously. 'Funny, I wouldn't have thought you were the kind of person to have grown up with maids.'

He coloured. 'Well, no, as I say, this was my uncle . . . one of my uncles. I had a lot of uncles. Ours was a . . . well, quite widely extended family. And I'm afraid it has to be said that my father, and my father's side of the family . . . were an entire flock of black sheep.'

'Ah.' Mrs Pargeter looked balefully at the monkey. 'I thought you were going to get rid of that thing. Have you rung the zoo yet?'

'Well, erm, no.' Hedgeclipper Clinton rubbed his hands in awkward apology. 'The fact is, I have heard from people that, er, well, that zoos often haven't got room for unwanted pets.'

'Are you saying you haven't rung them?'

'Erm, well, not exactly *rung*, no. There's such a problem with abandoned pets, you know. Don't forget that slogan, "A dog is for life, not just for Christmas." '

'That is not a dog,' said Mrs Pargeter evenly. 'That is a monkey. What's more, it's not a pet — or at least it's not my pet. It is just something that was foisted on to me, left in my sitting room by a person or persons unknown.'

'So you're saying you don't want to keep it?'

'That, Hedgeclipper, is exactly what I'm saying. Read my lips.'

'Now I wouldn't want you to be hasty, Mrs Pargeter. It is a fact that monkeys can be trained to do many useful tasks. I mean, they have the advantage of being able to get into buildings through entrances that are too small for human beings. It is possible that in the course of one of your investigations you might find it helpful to have the assistance of —'

'For heaven's sake, Hedgeclipper, I am not Tarzan! Not even Jane. And I have never felt the lack of a monkey to help me in anything I have wanted to do!'

'No . . . No . . . Fine . . .' He tried another tack. 'Erm, of course, monkeys can also become very affectionate and loyal pets, you know.'

'I'm not even going to argue that point — though I do rather doubt the truth of it, actually. But let me tell you that since the death of the late Mr Pargeter I have survived remarkably well without emotional encumbrances in my life, and I don't propose to change that situation now — certainly not for the sake of a monkey!'

'Ah.' For a moment, the hotel manager seemed about to counter with another argument, but the vigour of Mrs Pargeter's tone persuaded him against the wisdom of this. 'Well, right.' He was silent for a moment as he prepared the best order for his next sentence. 'But I take it that means, Mrs Pargeter, that you would have no objection to *my* keeping Erasmus . . . ?'

'You! Hedgeclipper, for heaven's sake! What on earth do you want with a monkey?'

He bridled, and looked at her with some dignity. 'I have always had a great affinity with the species. The fact is that my immediate family — the family in which I grew up — was . . . well, I believe the vogue word for it nowadays would be "dysfunctional". My father was . . . away a lot, and my mother took advantage of his absences to . . . entertain rather a lot of other gentleman friends . . . "uncles" she called them, so far as I was concerned. It was very confusing for a young lad. Quite honestly, every day when I bunked off from school, I didn't know who I'd be coming home to.

'But there was one fixed point of stability in all this confusion. One of my "uncles", you see . . .'

'He stayed around and really looked after you, did he?' Mrs Pargeter gently prompted.

'No,' Hedgeclipper replied, resentful of the interruption. 'He only stayed around one night so far as I recall. And spouted all this nonsense about being very rich, and having a house full of maids and other servants. Probably all lies. But he did bring something with him . . .'

'A monkey?'

Again the hotel manager looked a little sour at having his narrative hurried. 'Yes, it was a monkey. A monkey called Erasmus. Not a marmoset like this one, as it happens. It was a red-backed squirrel monkey, but a creature of very rare sensitivity. We . . .' He gulped. 'A relationship developed between us . . . boy and monkey . . . a close bond, one could say.' Emotion threatened the evenness of his voice. 'Erasmus was the nearest I ever had to a parent, Mrs Pargeter. When he died, I went into decline for nearly two years.'

'How did that decline manifest itself?' she

asked, all solicitude.

'Robbery with violence mostly,' he replied.

'Oh, I am sorry.'

'And a bit of GBH. I got very wild, I'm afraid. It was round that period that I was given the nickname "Hedgeclipper" for . . . well, for obvious reasons.'

Mrs Pargeter seized on the cue. 'Yes, I've often wondered why exactly you were called —'

He chuckled. 'Use your imagination.'

She knitted her brow, but her imagination remained, as it always had before when this subject arose, not quite equal to the task it had been set. 'Could you be a bit more specific, Hedgeclipper?'

But he wanted to move on. His lapse into sentimentality had perhaps been unmanly. In a brusque, businesslike voice, he said, 'So, if you have no objection, I intend to keep this Erasmus as a pet . . . and, er, confidant.'

'What, here in the hotel?'

He looked uncomfortable. 'Well, see how we go. There is an empty suite on the first floor. He could have that.'

'Yes . . . You don't think other guests might object . . . I mean, to the sort of things he gets up to?'

'He won't get up to anything he shouldn't. A little darling like this hasn't got an antisocial bone in his body.'

'Really?'

Hedgeclipper Clinton's face took on a stern expression of political correctness. 'Mrs Pargeter, you're in serious danger of sounding like one of those people who's prejudiced against monkeys.'

'Well, there's a surprise.'

'Why?'

'Because I bloody am.'

Chapter Seven

Nigel Merriman's office off Victoria Street was neat and tidy without being lavish. The serried rows of files, the neatly aligned telephones, fax and word processor, the discreetly groomed and unobtrusive secretary, all bore witness to the meticulousness of their owner's mind. It was the office of any efficient solicitor. There was no suggestion that Nigel Merriman had ever specialized in anything other than the legitimate business of his profession.

And indeed he hadn't. The late Mr Pargeter, when considering lawyers, would have been appalled at the idea of employing a bent one. He had always had a great respect for the British legal system, and the particular quality of it that he admired was its elasticity. The point of having a lawyer on your side was not so that that lawyer could bend or change the law, but rather that he could find in existing legal precedent justification for more or less any action that was required.

The fact that the late Mr Pargeter's unavoidable absences from the marital home had been as few and as brief as they had was a testament to his principle of only employing the most skilful and highly qualified legal assistance. He had even at times engaged the services of the most eminent lawyer in the land, Arnold Justiman. So it went without saying that Nigel Merriman, as one of the late Mr Pargeter's protégés, had been trained to the highest level possible. He was extremely good at his job.

But his professional skills had not proved equal to the task of getting much more information out of Concrete Jacket. 'Of course I asked him,' the solicitor confided to Mrs Pargeter, 'but my client denies there's anything anyone would want to blackmail him about.'

She put down her tea cup on Nigel Merriman's desk and sighed in exasperation. 'But if Willie Cass appeared at his house in front of lots of witnesses demanding a payoff, Concrete must realize —'

'I know, I know. I have made all those points to him, but he still says there's nothing. Presumably he's afraid that, by admitting Willie Cass did have a reason to blackmail him, he's going to make himself look even guiltier.'

Mrs Pargeter nodded. 'That could be the reason. It's also possible that he's afraid of implicating other people.'

The solicitor nodded slowly, taking in the new idea. 'I hadn't thought of that, Mrs Pargeter.'

She sighed again. 'If only we could get someone to talk to him . . .'

This, however, was perceived as a slight on Nigel Merriman's professionalism. 'I *have* talked to him,' he said. 'We've known each other a long time. I like to think there's a good basis of trust between us. But, even so, he won't tell me any-thing.'

'Hm. Presumably the police aren't that worried what the blackmail threat was about. It's enough for them that a lot of people saw Willie Cass threatening Concrete and demanding money from him.'

'Yes. As is usually the case, so long as the police get a conviction, they're not that bothered about the detail. I'm afraid, Mrs Pargeter, it does look as if my client has been — as he himself might put it — very thoroughly stitched up.'

The solicitor spoke these words as if they put an end to the matter, but Mrs Pargeter was not so easily daunted. 'Well then,' she said with a sweet smile, 'it's up to us to unpick the stitches, isn't it, Nigel?'

The solicitor coloured at the intimate use of his Christian name. But he rather liked it.

Unpicking stitches from Concrete Jacket didn't prove easy. Mrs Pargeter arranged to visit him in Wandsworth Prison that afternoon, and deployed her full armoury of blandishment, cajolery and importunity. Unusually, however, these potent weapons were on this occasion without effect. Concrete was pleased to see her, was polite and amiable, but gave nothing. Whenever direct ques-tions about Willie Cass's murder arose, he clammed up.

Eventually, in exasperation, Mrs Pargeter ex-claimed, 'But don't you realize — if you don't do anything to save yourself, you're going to get sent down for a great many years.'

'If that's the way it's gotta be,' the builder responded doggedly, 'then that's the way it's gotta be.'

'But what about Tammy? What about the kids? What kind of a future are they going to have if you're put away for life?'

His face betrayed how much her words hurt, but he still didn't change his position. Concrete Jacket stayed silent.

A less positive personality would have been cast down by this lack of reaction. Mrs Pargeter, however, had always regarded a setback simply as a stimulus to renewed endeavour.

Maybe Hedgeclipper Clinton might know some way to get through to Concrete, Mrs Pargeter thought, as she arrived back at Greene's Hotel early that evening. Though she had never been privy to any detail of the varied projects undertaken by the late Mr Pargeter, she was aware that many of her husband's former colleagues had at times worked together. And that there had been amongst them a network of camaraderie, which might offer some recollected clue to the builder's secretive behaviour.

There was no one on Reception. As she had done the previous day, Mrs Pargeter crossed the foyer and knocked on the door of Hedgeclipper Clinton's office. Once again there was no response, and on this occasion she could hear through the door no murmured endearments, nor any chattering from Erasmus.

She felt an unaccountable dread as she turned the doorhandle, and the sight inside the office justified her premonition. The room had been ransacked — not systematically as if someone had been searching for something, but randomly as if some huge beast had been — literally — throwing its weight about.

Computers and telephones had been smashed, a wall-safe pulled bodily from its setting, light fittings ripped from the ceiling, and the furniture reduced to matchwood. Only two chairs had survived the onslaught, and on these, strapped with nylon cords, their mouths shut off by carpet tape, sat the hotel manager and one of his receptionists.

Mrs Pargeter rushed across to free the prisoners. Ladies first. With an apologetic shrug for the inevitable pain, she ripped the tape off the girl's mouth, then attacked the ropes that held her.

'What happened?' she demanded, but the girl was hysterical and could not form an answer. 'Don't you worry about a thing. I'll just get Mr Clinton free, and we'll find you a nice hot, sweet cup of tea,' Mrs Pargeter said soothingly.

The girl nodded through her tears, as Mrs Pargeter performed the same rough surgery on the tape across the manager's mouth.

Hedgeclipper was a lot more vocal than his underling 'He took Erasmus!' he screamed in fury. 'The bastard took Erasmus!'

'Don't fret. I'm sure the monkey won't come

to any harm,' Mrs Pargeter reassured meaning-
lessly. 'Now you just hold still while I get these
knots undone.'

By the time the manager was free, the receptionist had recovered sufficiently to make a prac-
tical suggestion. 'Shall I go and phone the police?'
she asked through the final spasm of her sobs.

Mrs Pargeter looked sharply across to check
Hedgeclipper Clinton's reaction. Her own attitude to the police was one of great respect and
admiration, but she knew there were certain occasions when it was simply not worth adding to
their already excessive workload.

Hedgeclipper's reaction revealed that this was
one of those occasions. 'No,' he said judiciously.
'I think we might be better advised to keep this
quiet. We do have to think of our guests. The
presence in the hotel of a crowd of noisy police-
men would be bound to disturb the more sensitive amongst them.'

The girl looked dubious. 'But, I mean, when
someone's caused this amount of damage to the
place, surely the proper thing to do is —'

'Oh, this isn't really much damage. No, absolutely no problem at all,' said her boss breezily.
'I'll get this little lot cleared up in no time.'

'Even so,' the receptionist continued pugna-
ciously, 'it's not just the assault on property —
there's also the assault on us.'

'He didn't hurt us much — just tied us up,
that's all.'

But she wasn't going to be fobbed off by that

kind of reassurance. The receptionist was a girl of her time, aware of her rights as a woman, and of the political ramifications of any form of violence against her sex. 'You may not mind being assaulted and tied up like that — I regard it as an actionable assault against my freedom as an individual — and as a woman.'

'Oh, come *on,*' Hedgeclipper pleaded.

But the girl was not to be so easily diverted. She turned for support to Mrs Pargeter. 'Surely you must agree that we should call the police?'

If, however, she'd been looking for female solidarity, she'd chosen the wrong ally. Mrs Pargeter had quite detailed views of her own on the subject of women's rights, but she was first and foremost a pragmatist. If Hedgeclipper Clinton was signalling that the police should not be involved, then she was sure he was doing so for very good reasons.

'No, no, I agree it would only upset the other guests,' she said airily.

The receptionist looked shocked to hear such political flabbiness from a member of the sisterhood.

'Maybe,' Mrs Pargeter continued, looking across at Hedgeclipper, 'if the young lady were offered some compensation for the appalling distress that has been caused her, she might see the situation rather differently . . . ?'

He caught on instantly. 'That's a good idea,' he said, moving quickly across to where the safe lay on the floor, and twiddling the knobs to open it.

'If you think you can fob me off with money to stop me complaining about an assault on my dignity as a woman . . .' the receptionist began.

But when she saw how much money her boss was offering for her silence, she allowed her words to trickle away. Reaching across to take the two folded fifties, she concurred that it probably didn't make sense to upset the guests.

'No, I think you're absolutely right,' said Hedgeclipper. 'So glad you see it my way.'

'A mature, adult response,' Mrs Pargeter agreed, as the girl moved across to the door.

With her hand on the handle, she turned back curiously. 'Funny he didn't take the safe, isn't it . . . ? Or try to break into it . . . ? Or steal something other than the monkey . . . ?'

Another fifty hastily thrust into her hand melted away her inquisitiveness. With the shrug of someone who knows which side her bread's buttered, the girl left the room, the events of the previous hour expunged permanently from her memory.

'So what was it, Hedgeclipper?' asked Mrs Pargeter when they were alone. 'Or should I say *who* was it?'

His face turned grim as he replied, 'It was Fossilface O'Donahue.'

Chapter Eight

Mrs Pargeter left Hedgeclipper Clinton on the phone, trying to get a lead on Fossilface O'Donahue's possible whereabouts, and went up to her suite. She needed to call Truffler Mason.

Her first surprise on entering the sitting room was that the monkey was there again. Exactly as he had been a couple of days previously. Erasmus was on the floor, with his chain once again anchored to the leg of the dresser. Once again he had managed to leave his marks — scratches and other, less salubrious, souvenirs — around his small circle of territory.

As soon as she came into the room, he rose up on his hind legs and strained towards her, chattering frantically. His behaviour would no doubt have been appealing to Hedgeclipper Clinton — or perhaps to any other marmoset-lover. It wasn't to Mrs Pargeter. Why is it that animals instantly recognize the human beings who find them most repellent, and immediately focus all their attention on those poor unfortunates? Some animal behaviourists claim the response arises from an atavistic conciliatory instinct; Mrs Pargeter reckoned it was sheer bloody-mindedness.

Still, she was in no mood to be distracted. The welcome news for Hedgeclipper, that his precious

Erasmus was safe, would have to wait until after she had spoken to Truffler. She opened her bedroom door.

It was then that she had her second surprise. And it was an even less appealing one than the rediscovery of the monkey.

As she opened the door, Mrs Pargeter found its frame filled with the huge bulk of a man in a grey suit. He was built like a harbour wall and, incongruously, wore a clown mask over his face. It was plastic with a red nose, huge melon-slice mouth, exclamation-mark eyes, and ginger ropy hair radiating out from its dome.

Mrs Pargeter didn't often scream, but she did this time. It wasn't fear, she tried to tell herself, just shock.

'Mrs Pargeter.' The monster's voice was deep, without intonation, and very scary.

What was worse, she realized with a little gulp of horror, he knew who she was.

'Don't worry,' the voice went on. 'I'll take the mask off.'

If this action had been designed to allay her fears, it could not have been less effective. The face which the removed mask revealed she had only seen once, in a magazine photograph, but she had no problem in recognizing who it belonged to.

Fossilface O'Donahue.

Mrs Pargeter screamed again.

Chapter Nine

She backed away, her eyes locked on to the re-actionless pebbles caught in the crags of his features. Fossilface O'Donahue waved the clown mask towards her. 'Don't you think this is funny, Mrs Pargeter?'

His voice was deep, and he spoke as if the words were too big and cumbersome for his mouth.

She managed to find enough voice to reply, 'No, not at all funny, actually.'

'And what about the monkey? Don't you find that funny either?'

Mrs Pargeter shook her head. Fossilface O'Donahue looked downcast. 'Well, that's a pity, isn't it? Pity I'm not giving you a jolly laugh, isn't it?'

'Yes,' she concurred, trying out of the corner of her eye to judge how far she was from the door and what her chances of escape were. They didn't appear to be good. The man was huge. His arms looked long enough to reach out and snatch her from the other side of the room.

Another of the Greene's Hotel Regency telephones stood on a small table, tantalizingly close. But even if she could reach it, there was no chance the thug would give her time to dial for help.

He moved one ponderous, threatening step towards her. 'We've never met before, have we, Mrs Pargeter?'

'No.' Her confidence and resilience were beginning to trickle back. 'Never had that pleasure.'

'No.' He nodded slowly. 'I tend to keep myself to myself, as a rule. Though of course I did have quite a lot of dealings with your late husband . . .'

'So I gather.'

'It has to be said . . .' he continued slowly, that Mr Pargeter and me did not always see eye to eye about everything . . .'

'Yes, I'd gathered that too.'

He advanced another step. Mrs Pargeter wilted in the face of his overpowering presence, but managed to hold her ground.

'No, Mr Pargeter and I did have our disagreements. He didn't always like the way I conducted business.'

Mrs Pargeter couldn't stop a defiant response coming out. 'My husband always did have very high standards.'

Fossilface O'Donahue gave another ruminative nod. Somehow the slowness of his approach, the evenness of his tone, made him seem more rather than less menacing. When the violence came, Mrs Pargeter feared, it would be sudden and entirely devastating.

'Yes, I suppose that would be the way he saw it.' The man sighed. 'I've just come out after a twelve-year stretch, you know, Mrs Pargeter.'

'Really? And where was that?' she asked affably.

'Parkhurst the bulk of it. Then they give me the last year in a Cat. C nick. Erlestoke. You know it?'

'I've heard of it. Never actually been there.' There was something incongruous about this cocktail party chit-chat.

'Been to Parkhurst?'

'Never been there either, as it happens.'

'No. Rough nick, Parkhurst. No place for a lady . . .'

'Right.'

'Or indeed for a very sensitive sort of man. I'm not a very sensitive sort of man. Never have been.'

'No, I rather got that impression.'

'*Though,*' he said, with a sudden surge of volume, 'there are some things that I'm very sensitive about.'

'I'm sure there are. I think that's true of most of us,' Mrs Pargeter babbled.

'For instance, I'm very sensitive about criticism . . .'

'None of us like being criticized.'

'And I'm also very sensitive about justice.'

'Oh, well, that's good news. We're very fortunate that the British legal system is one of the best in —'

'I'm not talking about the British legal system, I'm talking about justice! Tit for tat, eye for an eye, tooth for a tooth, know what I mean?'

'Oh yes, I certainly do.' Mrs Pargeter's mind was racing. What were the chances of Hedgeclipper Clinton suddenly coming upstairs to check

69

that she was all right? Pretty minimal, she reckoned. The last thought that would occur to him was that his assailant was still inside Greene's Hotel. No, he'd still be ringing round his other associates, trying to see if any of them had got a lead on the whereabouts of the newly released Fossilface O'Donahue.

She wondered if it was worth trying another scream. Didn't seem much point, really. The first two had prompted no reaction from the other guests. And there was always the danger that a scream for help might further enrage her adversary, and make him speed up his schedule of violence. No, all she could do was wait — without much optimism — to see what happened.

'There was some people, you know,' the thug went on, 'who reckon it was down to your husband that I got caught last time out and had to go to the slammer.'

'Really? Well, people do get the wildest ideas, don't they?'

'Yes. You see, generally speaking, your husband was very good about seeing to it the blokes what worked for him was well protected . . .'

'Oh?'

'You know, so's they wouldn't get nicked.'

'Right.'

'System fell down with me, though.'

'Oh dear.'

'I just done this bank job, reckoned there'd be a getaway car to whisk me off, but there wasn't one. Two Pandas full of the filth instead.'

'That was unfortunate.'

'Good choice of word. Yes, it was unfortunate, Mrs Pargeter, very *unfortunate*.' He rolled the word round on his tongue, as if he was hearing it for the first time.

'And was there any reason why my husband let you down, Foss . . .' She decided that perhaps he wasn't as familiar with — or keen on — his nickname as others of his acquaintances might be. '. . . Mr O'Donahue?'

'There was a reason — or at least something he'd see as a reason. He'd been very particular before this job that there wasn't to be no violence. None at all, he said, it wasn't necessary. But I know my own business, and I know you can make some things happen a lot quicker when you're carrying a baseball bat than when you aren't.'

'So you did use violence?'

'Yes.' He looked aggrieved. 'Not much. I mean, nobody got killed or nothing like that. I should think all three of them was out of hospital within six weeks . . . well, three months, any-way.'

'And you reckon that's why my husband can-celled your getaway car?'

He nodded.

'But you don't think he actually tipped off the police, though, do you? I mean, I'm sure he'd never do anything like that.'

Fossilface O'Donahue was shocked. There were limits to the bad he could believe, even of his enemies. 'Oh no, he never done that. No, I think the appearance of the Pandas at that moment was just bad luck. Some twerp living round there must've heard the alarm go, and called the old Bill.'

'I should think that's what happened, yes.'

He nodded yet again and moved another step towards her. Mrs Pargeter felt the force of his closeness like the repellent pole of a magnet, but just managed not to back away.

'Thing is, you get a lot of time to think when you're in the nick . . .'

'I bet you do, yes. Not a lot else to do, is there?'

'Think about justice . . . think about scores being settled . . . think about who's responsible for things what've happened . . . think about ways of evening up the odds a bit . . . think about making them what's guilty pay for what they done wrong . . .'

'Yes,' Mrs Pargeter gulped.

'And while I was in the nick, I thought a lot about me and your husband . . .'

'Oh, did you?'

'. . . and the rights and wrongs of what happened between us . . .'

'Mm?'

'So when I come out, I was dead keen to get to see the old man again.'

'Ah.'

'Imagine how disappointed I was to discover that, while I been inside, he gone and snuffed it.'

'Yes, well, I was pretty disappointed too,' Mrs Pargeter admitted.

'But then I thought: well, if he's not around, best thing would be for me to settle any outstanding business there might be . . . *with his widow.*'

She could not control a little, involuntary gasp.

'Which is why I'm here.'

'All right then.' She spread her arms wide in a gesture of surrender. 'Do whatever you've got to do — but do it quickly. Let's get it over with, eh?'

'Too right,' said Fossilface O'Donahue. He stood craggy and huge in front of her. 'Yes, I'll do what I come here to do.' He was silent for a moment. Mrs Pargeter closed her eyes and tensed herself for the first blow. 'I got to ask you something first . . .'

She half-opened one violet-blue eye. 'Yes. What is it?'

He cleared his throat. The sound, so close, was like a post-earthquake landslide. Then he spoke.

'Mrs Pargeter . . . can you find it in your heart to forgive me?'

Chapter Ten

Mrs Pargeter always found that a bottle of champagne eased most potentially sticky situations, and the rest of her conversation with Fossilface O'Donahue was not likely to be the most relaxed social encounter she had ever experienced, so she made the relevant call to Room Service. She asked her guest to wait in the bedroom while the waiter delivered the bottle; she didn't want Hedgeclipper Clinton to know that Fossilface was in the hotel until she had found out a little more about the thug's intentions.

His plea for forgiveness had sounded genuine enough, but she still wasn't quite sure. There was something about his manner that seemed to breathe psychopathology.

They sat down with an unconvincing air of cosiness either side of a highly polished table. On the floor across the room, Erasmus, exhausted by his attempts to escape, had fallen asleep.

Fossilface drained his first glass of champagne as if he was participating in a speed trial, and Mrs Pargeter politely topped him up again. 'Now tell me all about it,' she said comfortably.

'Well . . . the fact is . . .' he rumbled. 'I done wrong.'

'Yes, but after all that time in prison, surely

you can feel that you've paid your debt to society and that you're ready to start a new life?'

'That is certainly true, Mrs Pargeter, that is certainly true. But the fact is, I still done wrong to various individuals what haven't been paid back yet.'

'Paid back?' she echoed, slightly alarmed.

'Yes. Paid back in full for what I done them out of over the years.'

'Ah.'

'You see, when I was in prison, Mrs Pargeter, I had, like, a mystical experience . . .'

'Oh?'

'Which made me think about everything what'd happened in my life, like, hitherfrom . . . you know, like, up to that point in time . . .'

'Right.'

'I had, like, a convergence.'

'Did you?'

'Yes. Just like St Paul on the road to Domestos.'

'Ah.'

'One evening I was sitting eating my supper when this geezer, who was one of the real hard men in the nick — "Chainsaw Cheveley" he was called — don't know if you know him . . . ?'

'No,' Mrs Pargeter admitted.

'You got any sense, you'll keep it that way. Well, on this occasion I'd rubbed old Chainsaw Cheveley up the wrong way, and he grabbed hold of a jug of custard and he upturned it over my head . . . You ever had a jug of custard upturned over your head, Mrs Pargeter?'

'No. No. I haven't, actually.'

'Well, it's not pleasant, let me tell you, not pleasant. For a start, it was dead hot. I mean, most of the nosh you get in the nick is, like, lukewarm at best, but — just my luck — this custard was really steaming. And it poured down all over my eyes, so I couldn't see nothing. And I thought, Chainsaw Cheveley is not long for this life. I mean, nobody does that kind of thing to Fossilface O'Donahue and gets away with it. I reckoned I'd pick up one of the chairs — they was metal, tubular jobs — and bash the living daylights out of him. Probably mean another charge and a longer sentence, but I didn't care. You know, when my rag's up, I don't think about things like that, never have done.

'So I reached my hands up to wipe the custard out my eyes and . . . then it happened.'

'What happened?' asked Mrs Pargeter.

'It was like there was this yellowish, golden kind of light glowing round everything I saw.'

'Ah. Are you sure it wasn't just the custard?'

'No, no, it was different from that. It was like more sort of . . . what's the word? Urethral?'

'Ethereal?' Mrs Pargeter suggested.

'Yes, that's probably it. Anyway, everything, like, glowed golden and, through the custard, I seemed to hear this voice . . .' He paused, distracted by the memory.

Who was it?' she prompted. 'Chainsaw Cheveley?'

'Nah, nah, it was, like . . .' He looked a little sheepish. 'I know this sounds daft . . . but I reckon it was an angel.'

'An angel?'

'Yeah.'

'What did the voice say?'

'It said: "Fossilface O'Donahue, you done wrong. You been a bad person. You've hurt people. You've never had no sense of humour about nothing. You gotta make restitooshun." '

' "Restitooshun"?'

'Restitooshun,' he confirmed gravely.

'And you say this was an angel?'

'I reckon it was. I mean, I couldn't, like, see anyone, but I reckon it was an angel, yes.'

'You don't think it could have been just Chainsaw Cheveley having you on?'

He shook his head decidedly. 'No way. Chainsaw Cheveley's never been heard to utter a sentence of more'n two words. He couldn't have spouted all that lot, no way.'

'Ah. So what did you do?'

'Well, immediately, I shook Chainsaw Cheveley by the hand, and I said, "Thank you, mate, from the bottom of my heart." '

'And what did he do?'

'He hit me with his spare fist. He thought I was only shaking his hand to make a move on him, you see.'

'So what did you do then?'

'I turned the other cheek.'

'Really?'

'Yeah. And so then he punched me on that one, and all.'

'And you still didn't hit him back?'

'No way. From that moment I was, like, a changed man. You know, they say the leopard can't change his stripes, but that's exactly what I done. From that moment I decided I would devote the rest of my life to making restitooshun to those what I done wrong to.'

'How long ago did this experience happen?'

'Well, about three years, but I couldn't do nothing about it while I was still in the nick, like. I mean, I could make myself be nice to my fellow inmates, but I couldn't sort out none of the blokes outside. Mind you, I could make plans for what restitooshun I'd make once I was a free man again. I thought of all the people what I done wrong to.'

'Oh yes?'

'There's a lot of them. Your husband, like I said . . . Truffler Mason . . . Concrete Jacket . . . That Gary, the getaway driver . . . Keyhole Crabbe . . . do you know him?' Mrs Pargeter nodded, and Fossilface continued piously, 'They was all going to need some restitooshun. And Hedgeclipper Clinton, and all.'

'So was tying Hedgeclipper and his receptionist up part of the "restitooshun"?'

'Well, no, I haven't got on to *his* restitooshun yet. I'm still working on yours — or rather your husband's . . . if you know what I mean.'

She didn't, but she felt this wasn't the moment

to ask for an explanation. 'So what else have you been doing for the last three years?'

'I been working on changing my personality,' he replied.

'Oh yes. How did you set about doing that?'

He smiled proudly. 'I went to see the chaplain. Never had any of that God stuff when I was a nipper, so I got him to take me through the whole business, right from the start . . . you know, the Garden of Eton, the whole number, right up to the Crucifaction and the Reservation . . . And I got him to give me books to read.'

'What — like the Bible?'

'Well, yes, a few like that, but more of them was joke books.'

'Joke books?'

'That's right. Because, you see, it's like what the angel said. Not only had I done wrong, but also I never had no sense of humour. That's what distinguishes man from the animals, the chaplain said — a sense of humour.'

'Well, it's a point of view.'

'So I been working the last three years to build up my sense of humour.'

'From the joke books?'

'Yes.' He nodded with satisfaction, then coughed. 'Do you know the joke about the nervous wreck?'

'No, I don't believe I do,' said Mrs Pargeter.

Fossilface O'Donahue chuckled. 'This'll kill you, really will. Dead good, this one. I spent most of the past three years practising telling jokes, you know.'

'Did you?'

'Yeah. All right, so here goes.' He cleared his throat again. 'What lies on the bottom of the ocean and shivers?'

'Amaze me,' said Mrs Pargeter.

'A nervous wreck!' Fossilface O'Donahue pronounced ecstatically, and burst into a deep rumble of laughter.

Mrs Pargeter joined in politely, though she thought he might still have a little way to go in his joke-telling technique. Fossilface wasn't yet quite ready for the professional stand-up comedy circuit.

'It's good, isn't it?' he said. 'Dead good.' Mrs Pargeter smiled encouragingly. 'No,' he went on, 'the chaplain told me . . . you go about your daily life with a sense of humour and people are bound to warm to you.'

'I'm sure they will.'

'So that's what I've been working on — my sense of humour. Making sure that everyone who meets me leaves with a smile on their face.'

'What an appealing idea.'

'Mm.' He waved the plastic clown mask at her. 'I thought this'd give you a good laugh.'

'Oh.'

He looked disappointed. 'Didn't, though, did it? It seemed almost like you was scared of it, rather than amused by it.'

'Well, yes, of course all jokes depend for their

effect on the mood of the person they're told to, don't they?' she said judiciously. 'And the occasion.'

'Yeah. So, another time, if you was, like, in the right mood, you'd've thought this mask was dead funny?'

'Yes, I'm sure I would, Fossilface.'

The nickname had slipped out unintentionally. Mrs Pargeter held her breath for a second, waiting for the reaction, but was relieved to see a smile split his craggy features.

'Good. That's what I want to do, you see — leave people with smiles on their faces.'

'Very nice too.'

'My aim is to, like, suddenly appear from nowhere, do the restitooshun to the geezers what I done wrong to, then vanish off again.' He chuckled throatily. 'Sort of like the Loan Arranger.'

'Sorry?'

'That's another joke I learnt from one of the books while I was in the nick. This bloke, see, he goes to the bank, and there's this other bloke sitting at a desk with a black mask on . . . I mean, the bloke's got the mask on, not the desk.'

'Right.'

'And the bloke — this is the first bloke, I mean the one who come in — he says to another bloke — this is not the one sitting at the desk with the mask on . . .'

'It's a third bloke, in fact.'

'It is. You got it, right, a third bloke. Anyway, this bloke — the one who's come in — he asks

81

the other bloke — not the one with the mask on his desk, that is, the third one — he asks him: "Oo's that bloke over there?" This is the one with the mask he's asking about now, right?'

'Right.'

'So the other bloke — this is the third one now . . .'

'I'm with you.'

'He says: "That bloke's our Mortgage Department. He's the Loan Arranger!" '

Fossilface O'Donahue rumbled with laughter at his punch-line, and Mrs Pargeter too managed to summon up a little chuckle. 'Very good, very good.'

'Yeah, well, the trick with jokes,' he confided, 'doesn't lie in the joke itself . . .'

'Doesn't it?'

'No, it's not the jokes — it's the way you tell them.'

'Ah.'

'I been practising that, and all.'

'Oh, it shows, it shows.'

'Yes. You know, I'm really working on this sense of humour business.'

'So I can see.'

'And I'm going to use it in the way I make restitooshun to the people what I done wrong to.'

'Oh really?' said Mrs Pargeter, unable to disguise the edge of anxiety in her voice. She didn't relish the loose cannon of Fossilface O'Donahue's sense of humour coming anywhere near her.

'You bet. For instance, do you know what I done wrong to your husband?'

'No.' Mrs Pargeter wasn't sure that she actually wanted to know.

'I cheated him out of five hundred nicker.'

'Oh dear. Well, I'm sure he would have forgiven you for —'

'Oh no, he's going to get restitooshun for it all right — or, actually, *you're* going to get restitooshun for it.'

'Thank you,' Mrs Pargeter murmured weakly.

'In fact, you already got it.'

'Have I?'

'Yes. You are the proud recipient of the first bit of restitooshun what I done since I come out . . .'

'Lucky me.'

'. . . and you're the first one to experience the full effect of my sense of humour.'

'Really?'

'So what do you think of it, eh?'

Mrs Pargeter was perplexed. 'I'm sorry. I'm not quite with you. You'll have to explain.'

Gleefully, Fossilface O'Donahue did as he was requested. 'I done your old man out of five hundred . . . What's the slang for five hundred?'

It all became horribly clear. 'A "monkey"?' she suggested with resignation.

'Exactly,' a triumphant Fossilface confirmed.

Mrs Pargeter looked down at Erasmus, sleeping in his circle of debris on the carpet. 'Oh yes,' she said. 'Very amusing.'

Chapter Eleven

'The thought of Fossilface O'Donahue having developed a sense of humour,' said Truffler Mason heavily, 'is almost too awful to contemplate.'

'Right. I'm afraid he hasn't really caught on to the idea properly yet. I mean, I think that maybe he understands the general principle of humour, but he sure as hell doesn't understand what makes something funny.'

'No, he always did have a rather ponderous approach to . . . well, to everything, really.'

Truffler took a contemplative sip of his champagne. They were in the bar of Greene's Hotel, later the same evening. Having started drinking champagne, Mrs Pargeter saw no reason to stop. Fossilface O'Donahue had gone, and a touching reunion been effected between Hedgeclipper Clinton and Erasmus. The hotel manager was determined to protect the marmoset more rigorously in future.

Mrs Pargeter would not have dared to give the monkey away again, had Fossilface still been there. She had come to the conclusion that his mind worked in a very linear way, and could not deal with more than one idea at a time. While he was in the process of making his misguided 'restitooshun' to her, he couldn't think about the 'restitooshun' he was planning for anyone else. If Fossilface discovered that Erasmus had been returned to Hedgeclipper Clinton, he was quite capable of trussing the hotel manager up all over again.

But Mrs Pargeter couldn't help finding the thug's incompetence slightly endearing. 'I think he's doing it all for good motives,' she said to Truffler in a conciliatory tone. 'His heart's in the right place.'

'That's never been an acceptable excuse for anything,' the detective growled. 'Fossilface O'Donahue is trouble, whatever he does. And I think I'd rather have him making trouble from bad motives than honourable ones. When you're dealing with a dyed-in-the-wool villain, you know what to expect. Whereas you have no idea what'll be the next idiocy committed by a born-again Robin Hood.'

'Oh, come on, give him the benefit of the doubt.'

'A very unwise thing ever to give to Fossilface O'Donahue. There's nothing more dangerous than the zeal of the convert. They're all the same — alcoholics, divorcees, vegetarians, smokers, Catholics . . .' He shuddered. 'And villains who've seen the error of their ways are the worst of the lot.' Suddenly anxious, Truffler asked, 'Who else did you say he wanted to make "restitooshun" to?'

'He said there were lots, but certainly Gary,

Concrete, Hedgeclipper, Keyhole Crabbe . . . and, er, you.'

The detective snorted. 'I'd better warn the others.'

'It may be all right, Truffler. And I really mean it when I say that Fossilface will be acting from the best of motives.'

'Doesn't matter what his motives are, that guy's a walking disaster area. And he has this nasty habit of disappearing off the face of the earth, so you can never know where the next attack's coming from. No, we've all got to be on our guard, no question.'

Mrs Pargeter sighed. She knew there was no shifting Truffler when he got an idea fixed in his mind. 'Well, let's try to forget about Fossilface for a moment, and think what we're going to do about Concrete Jacket. It seems like it happened in another lifetime, but it was only this afternoon I went to visit him in prison . . . and got nothing out of him.'

'Hm.'

'Come on, Truffler, we've got to get this sorted.'

'If Concrete really won't give us anything, I don't see how we can.'

Mrs Pargeter drummed her fingers on the table. 'There's got to be a way.'

'But if he won't open up to *you*, I don't see —'

'He doesn't really know me that well. I mean, he likes me and respects me because of my husband, but I'm not, like, one of his really close buddies.'

'No. Did you mention the late Mr Pargeter when Concrete wouldn't talk?'

'Oh yes, I was totally shameless. Played the full "What about your loyalty to my late husband?" card. Nothing. No, either Concrete's protecting someone . . .'

'Or?'

'Or just very scared.' For a moment Mrs Pargeter was lost in thought. 'You know I was talking about me not being one of his really close buddies?'

'Uhuh?'

'Has Concrete got any really close buddies? I mean, anyone who might stand a better chance of getting something out of him than I would?'

'Well . . . Guy he always used to be very matey with . . . was Keyhole Crabbe.'

'Oh?' Even if it had not been so recently mentioned by Fossilface O'Donahue, the name would still have been very familiar. Keyhole Crabbe had been a significant cog in the late Mr Pargeter's smoothly functioning business machine. And had indeed since that time used his specialized skills to help Mrs Pargeter investigate a murder on a housing estate called Smithy's Loam.

'Yes,' Truffler went on. 'Those two worked together a lot over the years. They was as thick as . . . as thick as . . . as thick as two close mates can be,' he concluded discreetly.

'Really?'

The detective nodded. 'Those two go back a long, long way. If anyone could make old Concrete talk, it'd be Keyhole.'

A light of excitement glowed in Mrs Pargeter's violet-blue eyes. 'Well then, why don't we —'

'One small problem, though.'

'What?'

Truffler spread his hands wide in a gesture of defeat. 'Keyhole's inside — doing a twelve-year stretch.'

Mrs Pargeter sat back in disappointment and frustration.

'Mind you,' said Truffler Mason, a twinkle lightening his lugubrious eye, 'that'd present less of a problem to Keyhole than it would to most people . . .'

Chapter Twelve

In a cell in Bedford Prison the inmate on the top bunk stirred, alerted by a metallic scraping sound he heard from the direction of the door. 'What's going on?' he asked blearily, peering through the half-light.

'Sorry, didn't mean to wake you. 'Sonly me,' a voice replied from the gloom.

'You going out then?'

'Just nipping down the kitchen for a cuppa.'

'Oh, right.' Reassured, the inmate on the top bunk snuggled back under his covers. 'See you in the morning,' he mumbled into a yawn.

The practised hands of the man at the door eased a flexible metal probe along the narrow crack. He let out a little sigh as he felt it engage with the bolt. Gently he pressured it back till a soft click told him that the door was unlocked.

He slipped through on to the dimly lit corridor. Stowing the probe in his pocket, he took out a compact ring of picklocks, instinctively found the relevant one and locked the cell door behind him.

Then Keyhole Crabbe moved silently along the corridor to tackle his next obstacle, the door from his cell block into the main body of the prison.

Three minutes later he slipped out of the front gates of Bedford Prison, listening for the bolt to spring shut behind him. By now he had a prison officer's overcoat covering his prison uniform. Keyhole Crabbe moved out of the floodlit area and slid unobtrusively into the shadows that edged the prison walls.

Walking — almost weaving — towards him along the pavement was a man in dinner suit and black tie. The prisoner recognized the prison governor, returning from a Police Federation Masonic shindig in London.

'Evening, Governor,' said Keyhole Crabbe, with a jaunty half-salute to his temple.

'Evening,' the prison governor replied, and walked on. Then he stopped for a moment, fuddled and bemused. He felt sure he recognized that face from somewhere.

But by the time he turned round for a second look, the figure of Keyhole Crabbe had disappeared round a corner. The prison governor shook his head, shrugged, and continued on his way.

Gary's limousine was parked, as per arrangement, in a side street adjacent to the prison. 'Any problems?' asked Mrs Pargeter, as Keyhole Crabbe joined her in the back and Gary eased the car into gear.

'No, doddle,' Keyhole replied. 'I do it fairly regular, you know. Old lady gets lonely sleeping alone in that big bed.'

'How's she keeping?'

'Oh, great.'

'And the kids?'

'Terrific. Would you believe there's another one on the way?'

'Really? Congratulations. When's it due?'

'Oh, early days. Another five months to go.'

'That's great news. Do congratulate your wife too, won't you?'

' 'Course I will.'

'And how long have you got to go now?' Mrs Pargeter posed the question with delicate tact.

'Done seven years. Five more outstanding. Reckon I could be out in eighteen months, though — with good behaviour.'

'And that . . . won't be a problem?' This question was floated even more sensitively than the previous one.

Keyhole Crabbe looked at her with reproach. 'Mrs Pargeter, surprised you have to ask. Model prisoner, I am.'

'Yes. Yes, of course,' said Mrs Pargeter. 'Sorry.' Hastily, she moved the conversation on. 'By the way, did you hear that Fossilface O'Donahue was out?'

'Yeah, I heard.' Keyhole Crabbe shook his head ruefully. 'Also heard something about he was a reformed character.'

'Given up his evil ways, yes.'

'Heaven preserve us. If he's as unsuccessful at being a goodie as he was at being a villain, we've all got problems.'

'He is actually planning to repay his debt to all the people he reckons he's done wrong to. "Make restitooshun" is how he puts it.'

'Oh, blimey,' Keyhole groaned.

'And he's intending on each occasion to do it in some way that demonstrates his sense of humour.'

'His *what?* Fossilface O'Donahue's sense of humour? That's a contradiction in terms.'

'Well, he's apparently undergone a major transformation while he was inside. Now he claims he's got a real sense of humour.'

'I don't know whether I dare ask how it manifests itself . . .'

'I think he's actually got a bit of work to do on the fine tuning.' And Mrs Pargeter outlined to Keyhole Crabbe Fossilface's amusing attempt to repay the 'monkey' that he owed her late husband.

At the end of her narration, Keyhole groaned again. 'Oh God. And you say he actually mentioned me by name?'

' 'Fraid so. What does he need to make "restitooshun" to you for?'

The prisoner grimaced. 'He done the dirty on me few years back when we was doing a bank job. Locked me in one of the vaults when the rest of the gang scarpered. So I was waiting there when the police arrived. Dead embarrassing for me of all people, as you can imagine.'

'Why particularly for you?'

'Well, I'm supposed to be this ace escape merchant, aren't I? But Fossilface had nicked all my picklocks and other gear, so I couldn't do nothing.'

'But could you have got out of a bank vault even if you had got your equipment with you?'

Keyhole Crabbe shrugged lightly. ' 'Course I could.'

'So he certainly owes you something.'

'Oh yes. "Restitooshun." Dear God, I hate to think what form it'll take.'

'Maybe he'll just pay you some compensation money . . .' Mrs Pargeter suggested. 'Maybe he'll give up these elaborate ways of paying people back.'

'I'd like to believe you,' said Keyhole Crabbe gloomily, 'but once an idea gets lodged in old Fossilface O'Donahue's head, it takes a bloody road-drill to dislodge it.'

'Oh dear.'

He sighed. 'Well, I'll just have to wait and see what happens. I'll be on my guard, though. Who else is on Robin-bloody-Hood's hit-list?'

'Truffler, Hedgeclipper, Concrete and Gary certainly.'

'You and all?' said Keyhole to the chauffeur.

'Yes,' Gary confirmed with foreboding.

'What wrong did he do you then?'

'Sabotaged a getaway car I was driving. Could've been bloody nasty. I was lucky to escape in one piece.'

'So what kind of humorous "restitooshun" do

you reckon he's going to make you for that?'

Gary shook his shoulders, as if suddenly cold. 'I shudder to think.'

'Come on,' Mrs Pargeter urged comfortingly. 'No point in worrying about things till they happen, is there?'

'Where Fossilface O'Donahue's concerned,' said a doom-laden Keyhole Crabbe, 'I'm rather afraid there is.'

'It'll be fine,' Mrs Pargeter said blithely. She looked at her watch. 'Should be in London in a couple of hours. Don't envisage any problems that end, do you, Keyhole?'

'Nah,' he replied. 'Done Wandsworth lots of times, haven't I? This time of night screws'll be asleep, anyway. Think everyone's banged up, don't they?' And, his worries about Fossilface O'Donahue temporarily allayed, Keyhole Crabbe chuckled fruitily.

In a cell in Wandsworth Prison, Concrete Jacket lay wakeful and troubled on his bunk. Beneath him his cell-mate snored deeply.

There was a scraping noise at the cell door. Concrete tensed. As the sound continued, he eased himself off down to the floor, and picked up an enamel jug from the table. He raised it to defend himself as the door opened.

The outline of a man appeared in the doorway. Concrete Jacket moved forward aggressively and hissed, ' 'Ere, what the hell do you think you're —'

'Concrete, it's me — Keyhole.'

The jug was halted in mid-descent towards the intruder's head. 'Keyhole Crabbe?'

'Right.'

Concrete Jacket looked bewildered in the half-light as Keyhole gently closed the door behind him. 'What you doing here then? Got transferred down from Bedford, have you?'

'Nah,' Keyhole replied easily. 'Just needed to see you.'

A suspicious light came into Concrete's eye. ' 'Ere, this isn't an escape, is it?'

His visitor was appalled by the suggestion. 'Good heavens, no. Very risky business, escape.'

'Too right,' the builder agreed. 'Makes you a marked man, that does.'

Keyhole nodded. 'Oh yeah. Wouldn't catch me doing it. Serve your time like a good boy, no fuss, get your remission for good behaviour — that's my philosophy.'

'Yeah.'

'It's all right to nip out for kids' birthdays, wedding anniversaries, that kind of number — otherwise, you just got to knuckle down and do your bird.'

'Right.' Concrete Jacket nodded his endorsement of these Victorian values. He gestured to a chair and the two prisoners sat down. 'So what is it then, Keyhole? Great to see you, by the way.'

'You too, my son.' Keyhole gestured to the sleeping cell-mate, the rhythm of whose snores had not changed at all. 'All right to talk with, er . . . ?'

'Oh yeah,' Concrete replied. 'That one'd sleep through the Third World War.'

Keyhole Crabbe nodded with satisfaction and drew a half-bottle of whisky out of his coat pocket. His friend's eyes lit up. Two enamel mugs were quickly found and charged. They were clinked and gratefully sampled.

'Now,' said Keyhole Crabbe, 'it's about this Willie Cass business, Concrete . . .'

Chapter Thirteen

The first streaks of dawn were lightening the sky as Gary's limousine drew up outside the main gates of Bedford Prison. The back door opened and Keyhole Crabbe emerged.

'Sure you'll be OK?' asked Mrs Pargeter.

'No problem,' the prisoner replied with a grin. 'Dozy lot in here.'

'I can't thank you enough for what you've done.'

Keyhole grimaced wryly. 'Just sorry I couldn't get you more. Afraid Concrete really clammed up on me.'

'Well, I'm very grateful for what you did get.'

He dismissed this with a flip of the hand. 'Quite honestly, Mrs P., when I think of all the things your husband sorted for me, it's the least I can do.'

Mrs Pargeter smiled. 'He'd be very grateful to you, and all.'

'Good. Always valued Mr Pargeter's good opinion.' He gave a little wave. 'Cheers. See you around.'

'Bye-bye, Keyhole.'

He closed the door of the limousine and moved towards the main gate of the prison, reaching into a pocket for his picklock as nonchalantly as a commuter returning home after a day at the office.

'Good old Keyhole,' said Mrs Pargeter.

'One of the best,' Gary agreed. 'Honest as the day is long.'

They both watched fondly as he turned the picklock, opened the prison gates and slipped inside. Gary switched on the ignition and the limousine sped off towards Greene's Hotel.

'Wonder what's eating Concrete . . .' the chauffeur mused. 'Unlike him not to confide in his old mate Keyhole.'

'Yes, I'd hoped we'd get more. Still, at least we've got those two names.'

'The blokes Concrete thought might be involved?'

'Right. Did either of them mean anything to you?'

Gary shook his head.

'Never mind,' said Mrs Pargeter comfortably. 'I bet Truffler'll know who they are.'

Keyhole Crabbe's cell-mate still breathed evenly, enjoying the sleep of the innocent (well, the damned-nearly-innocent-if-he-hadn't-been-stitched-up, in his case). Keyhole undressed quietly, and reached down to pull back the covers on his lower bunk.

There was a large paper-wrapped box on the bed.

He pulled the box out and looked at it in the pale light of the bluish overhead bulb that stayed on all night. The paper was blue- and silver-striped gift wrapping. A card with a picture of a pink hippopotamus was attached.

Keyhole opened the card, and, his eyes straining in the half-light, saw stamped at the top a round smiley-face logo. Beneath it was printed:

WHAT DO YOU SAY WHEN YOU ARE STOPPED BY A POLICEMAN?
I DON'T KNOW. WHAT DO YOU SAY WHEN YOU ARE STOPPED BY A POLICEMAN?
POLICE TO MEET YOU.

'Oh no . . .' Keyhole murmured.

With a sense of doom, he tore the paper off the box, and opened it.

Inside, neatly laid out, were a set of files in graded sizes, a selection of hacksaws, a hammer and a variety of cold-chisels, a crowbar, a packet of plastic explosive and an oxy-acetylene lamp. Wrapped round the handle of the hammer was a note. Unhappily, Keyhole flattened it out, and read:

NOW YOU'LL NEVER HAVE THAT LOCKED-IN FEELING AGAIN. APOLOGIES — IT WAS ALL MY VAULT!

Keyhole groaned. Fossilface O'Donahue's 'restitooshun' couldn't have been less appropriate. And after all the care he'd taken to keep his own probes and picklocks hidden . . . If the warders found a single item of that lot, he could wave goodbye to any thoughts of his sentence being reduced for good behaviour. Particularly if they found the plastic explosive. He'd be lucky to get away with only seven years added.

Wearily, he packed everything back into the box, and once again got out his metal probe to open the cell door.

The next morning, when the manager of the Bedford branch of the National Westminster Bank opened one of the vaults, he had no explanation for the gift-wrapped box of escaper's tools he found there.

Truffler Mason's filing system was of a piece with the rest of his office — antiquated and furry with dust. Shoeboxes, their corners reinforced with brittle, orangey sellotape, weren't up to the task of containing the profusion of photocopied sheets and fading photographs clinched together by rusty paper clips.

This archive was not catalogued on anything so mundane as an alphabetical system, but by an arcane method comprehensible only to its creator. No one but Truffler himself could have flipped through the desiccated pages with such speed and certainty to home in on the relevant dossier and hand it across the desk to Mrs Pargeter.

She stared down at the mugshot. The mug in question looked like a primary-school child's first incompetent effort with modelling clay.

'Blunt,' said Truffler. 'Called Blunt he is.'

Mrs Pargeter scanned the accompanying sheet. 'There's no first name down here.'

'Never had one. Only got the one name. Always just called "Blunt".'

'Any reason why?'

'As in "instrument." '

'Ah.' Mrs Pargeter looked more narrowly at a face which appeared to have been left too close to a fire and melted. 'Certainly suits him,' she observed, before turning back to the notes. 'Seems he's used a good few blunt instruments in his time, and all.'

Truffler screwed up his face. 'Oh yes. Nasty bit of work. Not of the subtlest either, when it comes to covering his tracks. Spends his whole life in and out the nick. You never met him, did you?'

Mrs Pargeter looked ingenuously at the detective. 'Why on earth should I have done?'

'Well, in the early days he worked quite a bit for Mr Pargeter . . . you know, back round the Basildon era.'

"Really?' said Mrs Pargeter, glacially innocent. 'My husband never talked to me about his work, and introduced me to very few of his colleagues.'

'No, of course not,' Truffler said hastily.

'It is only since his death,' she continued demurely, 'that I have used the address book he left me to make some . . . very useful contacts.'

'I understand completely.'

Truffler relaxed a little at the sight of a smile on Mrs Pargeter's lips, as she went on, ' "You don't want to worry your head about my business, Melita," he used to say to me . . .'

'Too right.'

' "Besides, what you don't know . . ." ' she smiled sweetly, ' ". . . you can't tell anyone else about, can you?" '

'He was a very shrewd man, Mr Pargeter,' Truffler asserted, then continued with diffidence: 'Incidentally, Mrs Pargeter, you remember . . . Streatham?'

Her face clouded. 'Streatham? I believe it's a South London suburb between Brixton and Mitcham.'

'No, you know what I mean. Streatham. Julian Embridge Streatham.'

The mention of the name sent darkened clouds over Mrs Pargeter's habitually sunny face. 'I thought we had dealt with that problem. Julian Embridge is currently serving a very long jail sentence — which is an inadequate revenge for what he did in Streatham, but better than nothing.'

She referred to an unhappy incident in her husband's generally successful career, when betrayal by a trusted lieutenant — the same Julian Embridge — had caused him a longer absence from the marital nest than either of them would have wished for. Though, as Mrs Pargeter mentioned, she had since exacted her revenge, the memory of Embridge's perfidy could still cause her anguish.

Truffler elaborated. 'Reason I mentioned Streatham is —'

He was interrupted by a sudden scream of Welsh anger from the outer office, and shrugged apologetically. 'Sounds like Bronwen's husband — ex-husband I should say — is back from Mauritius and has just phoned her up.'

Their ensuing dialogue was punctuated by further vituperation from the valleys. Through the wall they could not distinguish the words, but when a tone of voice is that expressive, who needs words?

'What were you saying about Streatham?' Mrs Pargeter prompted.

Truffler sighed ruefully. 'Just that there's little doubt that *he* . . .' a large finger prodded the photograph of Blunt, '. . . was in it right up to his neck.'

Mrs Pargeter looked grim. 'Right. So I have the odd score to settle with Blunt, don't I?' An even louder scream of Welsh fury thundered through the partition. Mrs Pargeter raised an eyebrow to Truffler, then asked, 'What about the other name Concrete mentioned?'

'Yes. Clickety Clark . . .' His hands instinctively found the relevant dossier and passed it across the desk. As he did so, Truffler shook his head in puzzlement. 'Odd. I mean, Clickety was in a totally different part of the business.'

'Still worked for my husband, though?'

'Oh yes, but he didn't do no heavy stuff.' Mrs Pargeter gazed at the detective with charming incomprehension. What on earth could he mean by 'heavy stuff'?

'He done photography,' Truffler explained. 'Passport photographs, that kind of number, anything photographic where sort of . . . specialized work was needed. We used to call him "Wandering Hands".' Mrs Pargeter looked at him for elucidation. 'Because he was always touching everything up.'

'Ah.'

'What old Clickety's doing now, though, I've no idea. I think we should —' He was interrupted by the sound of a heavy object being hurled with some force at the dividing wall between the two offices. 'Excuse me a moment, Mrs Pargeter.'

With the long-suffering weariness of someone who has gone through these motions many times before, Truffler Mason rose to his full length and crossed to a dusty cupboard. He unlocked it to reveal shelves piled high with brand-new plastic-wrapped telephones. He took one out and turned to face the door.

As he did so, a diffident tap was heard, and the door opened. Bronwen stood there, flushed and apologetic. In her hands were the tangled remains of a smashed telephone.

Wordlessly, Truffler took the debris and handed her the new one. Bronwen smiled embarrassed gratitude and went back to her desk, closing the door behind her. Truffler chucked the shattered telephone into the bin.

With no reference to the incident, he then said, 'Right, Mrs Pargeter. I think we need to get some up-to-date info on Blunt and Clickety Clark.'

'And how are we going to do that?'

'We are going,' said Truffler with a foxy grin, 'to visit the offices of *Inside Out.*'

Chapter Fourteen

The offices of *Inside Out* were housed in Swordfish Wharf, a gleaming new tower block in Docklands. 'Not a million miles from Wapping,' Truffler Mason observed, as Gary's limousine deposited them outside the entrance. 'They say that's the new Fleet Street, don't they?'

'The only people who say it are people who haven't been here,' said Mrs Pargeter, looking up with distaste at the glass box that loomed above them. 'The only journalists I've met recently say nothing will replace the old Fleet Street.'

'Ah, but where did you meet them, Mrs P.?' asked Truffler, as they crossed a foyer, whose copious vegetation was apparently trying to reproduce an air-conditioned rainforest. The steel sculpture of a swordfish rising out of the green looked confused by its alien environment.

'Boozing in pubs round Fleet Street,' she replied. While they waited by the over-designed slate-gray counter for one of the uniformed security men to get off the telephone or stop staring portentously at his monitor screen, Mrs Pargeter indulged in a moment of nostalgia. 'No, these days they're trying to get rid of all the old stereotypes. Proper, heavy-drinking journalists are being replaced by Perrier-swilling suits who never leave their keyboards. Television producers now sit around earnestly thinking of minority interests and sipping nothing stronger than a large *espresso*. Do you know,' she concluded on a note of awe, 'nowadays apparently there are even teetotal publishers?'

Truffler Mason shook his head and grinned. 'Still, you'll never go that way, will you, Mrs P.?'

'I should think not!' she replied indignantly. 'I'm not a religious person, but clearly whoever devised this world we live in filled it full of delightful treats — food and drink being high on the list. And not to take advantage of that divine generosity — whatever creed you may happen to believe in — amounts to downright blasphemy, so far as I'm concerned.'

'Too right,' Truffler nodded. 'Too right.'

One of the security men had disengaged himself from the telephone. He looked up at them balefully. 'Can I help you?' he asked unhelpfully.

'The names are Mason and Pargeter.'

'Oh yes?' His tone was heavy with disbelief.

'We've come to see Ricky Van Hoeg,' Truffler continued. 'He is expecting us.'

'Really?' This appeared to the security man an even less likely assertion. He punched some numbers vindictively into his telephone. After a brief conversation, he was forced grudgingly to concede that they were expected.

He thrust a clipboard towards them. 'Fill in your names, companies represented, whom visiting, time of arrival, estimated time of departure, name of insurance company, telephone contact number for next of kin, and nature of business. Then the computer will issue you with a visiting number which you wear in *this* plastic badge. Do not remove your visiting badge at any time while you are within the building, and return it to the desk here on departure. Under no circumstances change your visiting badge with anyone else — it is *not* transferable.'

Mrs Pargeter fixed the security man in the beam of her violet-blue eyes. 'I don't really think we want to bother with any of that,' she murmured sweetly.

The security man shrugged. 'Oh, well, please yourself,' he said, and, as they crossed to the lifts, he turned back to watch his security monitor, which was showing a mid-morning cookery programme. He made notes on a pad of the ingredients for *mangetouts au gratin à la provençale*.

The lift doors opened and an infinitely tall, infinitely thin woman emerged. She had the contours of a stick insect, and was dressed in designer clothes that would be the envy of stick insects all over the world. She looked fabulous.

'Mrs Pargeter!' she exclaimed in hearty Cockney, and swept the shorter, fatter woman up into her arms.

'Ellie!' Ellie Fenchurch was the country's most vitriolic celebrity interviewer. Her Sunday newspaper column made compulsory reading for anyone who enjoyed seeing the great and good humiliated (and that, of course, included just about everyone). Talentless and graceless minor royals, devious cabinet ministers, testosterone-choked sports heroes, oversexed rock stars, unfaithful newsreaders, and supermodels whose braincell count didn't reach double figures — they had all had cause to smart from the interviewing technique of Ellie Fenchurch. Which made all the more remarkable the huge and continuing queue of celebrities desperate to be given the same treatment.

As they disengaged from the hug, Mrs Pargeter said, 'You know Truffler, don't you?'

' 'Course I do.' Ellie was exactly the same height as the detective. She enthusiastically kissed the air to either side of his cheeks.

'What you doing here then?' asked Mrs Pargeter.

'My office is here, isn't it?'

'Is it? I thought you worked for one of the Sundays.'

'I do. And that's based here.'

'Oh, I see, so there're legitimate papers here, and all, are there?'

Ellie's brow wrinkled. 'What do you mean — legitimate?'

Truffler clarified the situation. 'We're coming to see Ricky Van Hoeg at *Inside Out*. I think Mrs Pargeter may have somehow got the impression that it isn't a legitimate publication.'

'What, you mean it *is?*' asked Mrs Pargeter innocently.

' 'Course it is. Everything comes under the Swordfish umbrella,' said Ellie.

'But I thought it was called the Lag Mag for prisoners and —'

'It is. That doesn't mean it's not legit, though. There's a market out there. Swordfish Communications are very shrewd operators. They'll publish a magazine about *anything*, so long as they can make money out of it. Isn't that right, Truffler?'

He nodded. 'You bet. They do *Knicker-Nickers' World* . . . and *Mom's Dancers' Monthly* . . .'

'*The Ferret-Fanciers' Gazette* . . .'

'*Which Depilatory?* . . .'

'*Matchstick Modelling Today* . . .'

'*The Cribbage Quarterly* . . .'

'Oh yes,' Ellie Fenchurch concluded. 'Swordfish magazines'll explore any niche market there is. You see, the thing about ferret-fanciers or matchstick-modellers is: there may not be that many of them, but, by God, they're loyal. Circulation guaranteed to stay steady. All the same articles get recycled — with slight editorial adjustments — every three or four months, production costs are pared down to the bone, but, in spite of all that, the punters just keep on buying.'

Mrs Pargeter looked bewildered. 'I thought Swordfish was about the big newspaper titles — the daily and the Sunday one. That's what they're known for, surely?'

Ellie Fenchurch shook her head. 'Don't you believe it. Those're the public profile, yes, but they both make a big loss. Swordfish's profit comes from the advertising it sells for local papers and the specialist markets. I mean, if you're trying to sell protective underpants for people who want to do ferret-down-trouser tricks in pubs, there's not many places you can advertise, is there? Got to be *The Ferret-Fanciers' Gazette*, hasn't it?'

'I suppose so.' Mrs Pargeter smiled. 'What're you up to at the moment, Ellie?'

'Right this minute, I'm just off to do a character assassination on an Australian soap opera star.'

'Oh, nice.'

'Well, *I'll* enjoy it. But that won't take long. Once he knows I know about his very close interest in sheep, I think the interview could come to an abrupt end. How's about lunch? You not going to be with Ricky all day, are you?'

'Hour, maybe,' said Truffler.

Ellie Fenchurch looked at her watch. 'Great. See you both at the Savoy Grill half past one. We'll all get thoroughly rat-arsed.'

'But, Ellie,' said Mrs Pargeter ingenuously, 'I didn't think journalists drank these days.'

'No, of course they don't.' Ellie Fenchurch let out a snort of laughter. 'And, what's more, politicians don't take backhanders!'

Chapter Fifteen

These days, Mrs Pargeter thought regretfully as she and Truffler were ushered into the presence of *Inside Out*'s editor, even journalists' offices don't look any different from anyone else's offices. The huge floorspace covering a whole storey of Swordfish House, the rows of open-plan low-walled cubicles, each centred on the winking coloured screen of a computer, could have belonged equally convincingly to a bank or a mail-order firm or an insurance company.

What she thought of as the hack's natural environment — battered manual typewriters, overspilling wicker wastepaper baskets, encrusted coffee cups with cigarette butts floating in them, a half-bottle of whisky in the bottom desk drawer, and maybe even the odd green eye-shade — had vanished for ever. Journalism had followed the route of so many professions, hands on human contact giving way to a life lived by remote control, its reality distanced from its operators through the medium of the microchip.

Dear oh dear, thought Mrs Pargeter, not like me to be so maudlin. She pulled herself together with the memory of some words the late Mr Pargeter had often spoken to her. 'Everyone should home in on what they're good at, Melita my love. You're good at being positive. So be positive. There are quite enough people out there who're good at being negative, but what you've got going for you is something much rarer.'

She smiled at the recollection as she leant forward to shake the hand of Ricky Van Hoeg, editor of *Inside Out*. His superior status over the other hacks at least gave him the right to a small cubicle in the corner of the office, but its glass walls and open door did not make it seem very separate from the hushed, open-plan keyboard-clacking environment outside.

Ricky Van Hoeg was in his thirties, earnestly bespectacled, with the look of someone whose life mission it is to sell you a mortgage. Mrs Pargeter wasn't sure what she was expecting — or even wanting — but it wasn't this. She would have hoped that the editor of a prisoners' whereabouts magazine might have some minimal element of loucheness about him.

But Ricky Van Hoeg showed not a flicker of the unconventional. He had, she later discovered, started working for a property company's house magazine, then moved across to Swordfish Communications as a sub-editor on *Dentifrice and Floss Monthly*. From there he'd been promoted to deputy editor of *Morris Dancers' Monthly*, and recently moved to take over *Inside Out*.

He spoke about his job with pride but without humour. He showed his guests the mock-up for the next month's cover. There was a glossy colour photograph of Wormwood Scrubs gates. Contents promised inside included: GATE FEVER: IS IT ALL IN THE MIND?, HOW TO ORGANIZE A COMING-OUT PARTY, AMATEUR DRAMATICS FOR A CAPTIVE AUDIENCE, MAKE YOUR PIN-UPS REALLY LAST — TRY SHRINKWRAPPING, as well as regular features — NEWS OF THE SCREWS: WHICH ONES'VE BEEN TRANSFERRED WHERE?, THE GOOD NICK GUIDE — WINSOME GREEN, plus of course our invaluable listings: WHO'S IN WHERE, HOW LONG, WHAT FOR, AND DID THEY DO IT?

'All going all right then, Ricky?' asked Truffler after they had shown proper appreciation for the mock-up.

'Excellent. Circulation on the up and up.'

'Well, stands to reason. When you've got a prison population that's going up and up . . .'

Ricky Van Hoeg gave the detective a narrow look. He didn't want his achievements underestimated. 'Our circulation is going up at a faster rate than the prison population,' he said coldly.

Mrs Pargeter instantly defused any potential atmosphere between the two men. 'Obviously means you're doing a very good job, Ricky.'

'I like to think so. Anyway, what can I do for you, Mr Mason?'

'It's a touch of the old *quid pro quo*,' Truffler replied. 'You remember, I helped you out with some info on the Machete Murders Retrospective you done?'

'Yes, of course. And very useful it all turned out to be.'

'Good. Well, now I need a bit of gen on a

couple of lags, and I thought you'd be the geezer to help out.'

'No problem. We have a variety of research resources here at *Inside Out*. If we have serious difficulty in finding out about people, we put out requests for information on the Internet. That's proved very successful. But let's start with the basic, shall we?' Ricky Van Hoeg turned to his computer and deftly punched at the keyboard. Rapidly changing images flickered across the screen. 'Are the people in question actually inside at the moment?'

'No, no, both very much on the loose. That's why we need to know about them.'

'What're their names?'

'Well, what I've got're kind of, like, nick-names . . .'

'We have people listed on the database with their *noms de guerre* as well as their real names. Some of their aliases run into the hundreds, but . . .' Ricky Van Hoeg continued with the smug pride of a bank manager unveiling a new savings account, '. . . we can run a search according to any parameters you care to specify and find them within seconds. So what're the names?'

'Clickety Clark and Blunt,' said Truffler.

Ricky Van Hoeg immediately keyed in the information. The screen split down the middle. Two photographs appeared. They were not the same poses as those Truffler had produced, but their subjects were easily recognizable.

Below Clickety Clark's picture was the record

of an eighteen-month stay in Lewes Prison for forgery of a Buckingham Palace security pass a few years previously. 'Ah,' said Mrs Pargeter fondly, 'just after my husband passed on.'

Truffler nodded. 'Yeah, a lot of them went off the rails round that time. Without Mr Pargeter's good sense and guidance, some come horribly unstuck.'

Mrs Pargeter did not allow herself to get misty at the recollection. 'But look at Blunt's record! Now that is what I call "form"!'

It was indeed a very full criminal *curriculum vitae*. The wonder was, given the closeness of the sentences, how Blunt actually found the time to commit the crimes for which he was so regularly sent down. Not that his recent convictions were for major crimes. In fact, for someone with such an awesome reputation in the Grievous Bodily Harm department, they were little more than peccadilloes. Stealing cars, trashing restaurants, handling stolen videos, purloining credit cards — these were the currency of the petty criminal. The only assault on a human being Blunt had committed in the previous three years was whacking one barman in a pub, and even then the victim had only lost two teeth.

'Seems to have gone soft in his old age,' said Mrs Pargeter.

Truffler, who had had the same thought, nodded and said judiciously, 'Well, that was probably *his* way of going off the rails when your old man died.'

That got a rather piercing look from the violet-blue eyes, so he moved quickly on. 'This is great, Ricky.'

'Anything else you need? Only . . .' the editor took a none-too-discreet look at his expensive watch, '. . . I've got to see someone at the Home Office about getting *Inside Out* on to their regular distribution list for all staff. I think the deal's in the bag, mind you, and that could be another very healthy boost to circulation.'

'Yes, I'm sure,' said Mrs Pargeter.

'No, that's great, Ricky,' said Truffler. 'Thanks for your help. If it'd be possible to have a printout of the info . . . ?'

'No problem.' Ricky Van Hoeg pressed a key and, in seconds, Clickety Clark and Blunt's details were printed out in colour. The photographer's fitted on to one sheet; Blunt's ran to seven.

In the lift, Mrs Pargeter asked Truffler what his next step in the investigation would be.

'Try and find out what's really been going on inside the nicks.' He grinned mournfully. 'Stan the Orang-Utan's been inside for a while. He's the kind of bloke who keeps his ear to the ground. Might have a word with his boy.'

Mrs Pargeter had never heard of Stan the Orang-Utan, but her discretion was far too finely tuned for her to ask any embarrassing questions, like how he had got his nickname. Instead, as they emerged from the lift into the foyer of Swordfish House, she observed to Truffler what a boring man she had found Ricky Van Hoeg to be. 'I mean, I'm sure, back in the old days, people connected with crime had a bit of colour and glamour about them . . .'

'Ah, but he's not connected with crime, you see, Mrs P. He's a pukka, legit journalist, isn't he?'

'Well, mind you, in the old days, pukka legit journalists had a bit of colour and glamour. Never mind . . .' A smile spread across her plump, comfortable features. 'We're going to have lunch with one of the few who still has.'

They hailed a cab to the Savoy Grill. And, as Ellie Fenchurch had promised, they all got thoroughly rat-arsed.

Chapter Sixteen

On the rare occasions that she did get thoroughly rat-arsed, there was nothing Mrs Pargeter liked better than to work off her intoxication with a little lavish shopping. Some of the best purchases of her life had been made when mellow with alcohol, and she was very pleased with the haul she made that afternoon. She also found, as always, that an hour or so's vigorous workout with the credit cards had the effect of clearing her head completely.

The limousine was parked outside Greene's Hotel under the approving eye of a doorman who would instantly have moved on a vehicle containing anyone other than Mrs Pargeter. Gary, loaded down with Harrods carrier bags, followed his employer into the foyer.

'Hedgeclipper's really had this place done lovely, hasn't he?' the chauffeur observed, as they crossed the black and white marble floor. 'Strikes me every time I come in here.'

'Oh yes, he always did have a good eye,' Mrs Pargeter agreed.

The object of their compliments, immaculately dressed in black jacket and pinstriped trousers, was standing behind the elegant antique desk which served as the Greene's Hotel Reception.

The only out-of-place element in his *soigné* image was once again the marmoset perched affectionately on his shoulder. Gary opened his mouth to make some comment on this, but was stopped by a slight shake of his employer's head.

Hedgeclipper Clinton beamed at his most favoured guest. 'What a lovely afternoon, Mrs Pargeter.'

'Indeed. And how's Erasmus behaving himself?'

The hotel manager shook his head and tufted. 'He's been a little tinker this morning, I'm afraid. Smeared an orange all over my William and Mary walnut chair. Still . . .' he went on with an indulgent shrug, 'not a lot one can do about it, is there?'

Gary's instinctive answer to this too was prevented by a look from Mrs Pargeter. Instead, the chauffeur nodded amiably to his former colleague. 'Just saying you done a lovely job here, Hedge—' A look from the hotelier froze off the second half of the word. 'Mr Clinton,' Gary corrected himself.

Mr Clinton was once again wreathed in smiles. 'Thank you so much. I'm delighted you like it. And all well with you, Mrs Pargeter?' he asked solicitously.

'Fine, thank you.'

'No more trouble, I trust, from Fossilface O'Donahue?'

'Not a squeak out of him. Seems to have once again vanished off the face of the earth.'

'Good, I'm so pleased to hear that. Let's hope things stay that way,' Hedgeclipper Clinton said as he pressed an unseen button for the lift doors to open. 'And, though it's perhaps selfish of me, may I say that I do hope that dream house of yours isn't coming along too quickly. Greene's Hotel doesn't like to lose a guest of your calibre, Mrs Pargeter.'

She grimaced wryly. 'Have no worries on that score. Whatever the house is doing, it certainly isn't coming along too quickly.'

As the lift rose, Gary continued his musing about the success of Greene's Hotel. 'No, Hedge-clipper really knows what's what. Got taste, that's what it is, taste. Anyone who was taught by your husband really learnt the lot. I mean, there's no way Hedgeclipper could be running a place like this without what Mr Pargeter done for him. No way I could be doing the car-hire business.'

'Any more bookings, by the way?' asked Mrs Pargeter, always concerned about the health of Gary's business.

'Just rung Denise,' he replied with satisfaction. 'Got a wedding this weekend.'

'Great.'

'Someone she knows. Local too, so that's good. No, excellent thing to get into, weddings. Want a bit more of that kind of business.' He was silent for a moment. 'I'm thinking of buying something old for the weddings.'

'How do you mean — something old?' asked Mrs Pargeter as Gary drew back the lift doors and let her out on to the landing.

'Old car. Roller, Bentley, something like that. Vintage touch. Lot of girls these days want to arrive in the church in something a bit classy.'

'Well, if you want a loan to buy the thing, you have only to say the word.'

'No, Mrs Pargeter, wouldn't seem right borrowing from you.'

'Wouldn't be borrowing. I'd regard it as an investment in your business.'

Gary shook his head. 'Kind of you, but no thanks. I'll save up what I need out of my profits. That's the best way.'

'If you're sure . . .'

' 'Course I am. Something your husband used to say to me quite often: "Neither a lender nor a borrower be." '

'Ah yes.'

'Always had a way with words, Mr Pargeter. Kept making up clever little sayings like that, you know.'

'Mm,' Mrs Pargeter agreed, a little wistfully.

They had reached the door to her suite. She opened it with her key and ushered the chauffeur inside. The sitting room bore not a single trace of the devastation Erasmus had wreaked on it. Gary neatly lined up the Harrods carriers on a luggage bench.

'Thank you so much for doing that.'

'Pleasure, Mrs Pargeter. And you'll call me when you next need the car?'

'Of course.' She looked at him with sudden

beadiness. 'By the way, Gary, you haven't sent me an invoice yet.'

He coloured. 'No, well, I —'

'Do it.'

'Yes, Mrs Pargeter,' he said meekly.

'Otherwise,' she continued, 'it's going to be a very long time before you can afford to buy that Roller.'

'Yes, yes, I know. It's just that I feel I owe you such a lot for —'

'I expect an invoice in tomorrow's post, Gary. If you don't collect what's owing to you, you'll never save any money.'

There was no arguing with that tone in Mrs Pargeter's voice.

'Of course not. 'Nother thing I always remember your husband used to say: "Look after the pennies and the pounds'll look after themselves." ' Gary looked envious. 'Wish I could come up with neat little things like that.'

'Don't worry,' Mrs Pargeter said kindly. 'We've all been blessed with different gifts. With my husband it was words . . .'

'Amongst other things.'

'Amongst other things, yes. With you, though, it's driving. My husband never actually passed his driving test, you know, so you've got the advantage of him there.'

'Yes. Yes, I have, haven't I?' The thought seemed to cheer him. He moved to the door. 'OK, give me a bell if you need me. And I'll see you get an invoice in the morning.'

' 'Bye, Gary. And if you change your mind about the loan for the Roller . . .'

The chauffeur shook his head, but with marginally less conviction than he had before. After he'd gone, Mrs Pargeter went through into the bedroom and looked benignly down at her late husband's photograph. 'You did a good job with that boy,' she said. 'Gary's heart's in the right place, no question.'

Suddenly she remembered something and hurried out into the sitting room. She came back, holding a bright silk blouse against her ample frontage, and again faced the photograph. 'Nice one, this, isn't it? Really *me,* as you always used to say. Don't ask the price, though. Can't run the risk of you having a posthumous heart attack, can we? You wouldn't believe the way things've gone up since you popped your clogs, love.'

She hung the blouse in the mahogany wardrobe, and was thoughtful for a moment. Then, turning back to the photograph, she mused, 'You know, I'm drifting on this Concrete Jacket case. No forward momentum. I think the time has come for me to *make* something happen.' Mrs Pargeter made a decision. 'Yes, this could be exactly the right moment to get things under way.'

She grinned. 'As you always used to say, love: "There is a tide in the affairs of men, Which, taken at the flood, leads on to fortune." '

'Hm,' she chuckled as she reached for the Yellow Pages, 'and no doubt Gary thinks you made up that one too.'

Chapter Seventeen

The two youths wore sleeveless T-shirts and the bulges of their biceps left no doubt that they worked out. Their blonded hair was as short as Velcro over their scalps, and though the only weapons they carried were wet rags and sponges, they looked menacing enough for the majority of motorists, whether they wanted their windscreens cleaned or not, to hand over the price of a quick getaway when the lights changed.

The younger youth swaggered across to the battered brown Maxi that drew up at the head of the queue just as the green light gave way to red.

'Do your windscreen, guv?' The voice was abrasive South London and what it said was a classic example of something Latin masters have spent many generations trying to din into their charges: a question expecting the answer Yes. Though in fact 'demanding' might be a more accurate description.

'And what if I don't want it done?' asked the driver, a mournful, long-faced man in a brown suit.

The youth flexed his threatening biceps and loomed over the Maxi as if he could crush it like a cigarette packet. 'Well,' he replied softly. 'I think you might regret that decision, guv. I'm sure you wouldn't like —'

But suddenly, as he recognized the driver, his whole attitude and body language changed. The beefy frame seemed to shrink into a posture of conciliation — even supplication — as he mouthed the name, 'Truffler'.

'Right. I've been looking for you.' The tall man leant across to open the passenger door. 'Get in, Seb.'

'But I —'

'Get in,' Truffler repeated in a voice that eliminated the option of refusal. The boy called Seb looked across at his fellow extortioner, shrugged helplessly and got into the Maxi's passenger seat. At that moment the lights changed to green and the car lurched forward.

After a few minutes of silence, Truffler asked, 'How's your dad?'

'All right,' the boy replied, his South London rasp giving way to the rounded vowels of a public school education.

'He's a good lad, Stan,' said Truffler. 'You keeping in touch with him, are you, Seb?'

'Oh yes. Saw him at Visiting on Sunday.'

'Last time *I* saw Stan,' Truffler ruminated, 'he said the one thing he cared about was that you didn't get into trouble with the law.'

'I'm not in trouble with the law,' Seb protested, perhaps a little too vehemently.

The older man's tired eyes flicked across at him. 'So what's with all this windscreen-cleaning business then?'

'That's not illegal . . . exactly.' But the boy's colour and hesitation showed he wasn't even convincing himself.

Truffler pursed his lips and drove on towards his office.

When she brought the coffee in, Bronwen looked with undisguised admiration at Seb's physique. 'You know,' she mused, to no one in particular, 'I often think the answer to my problems might be a toyboy . . .'

Seb grinned, but Truffler came back at her in a tone which, by his normally gentle standards, was harsh. 'Yeah? And I sometimes think the answer to your problems might be getting that filing finished.'

She pouted and looked round the office with mock despair. Certainly the prospect of filing the debris that covered every surface there was a daunting one.

'You know I don't mean in here,' said Truffler. 'This lot *is* filed.'

And it was, according to his system. The shoeboxes of papers he had gone through with Mrs Pargeter still lay piled over other layers on his desk, and the rest of the room looked as if a bomb had gone off in a paper factory. But to Truffler it all made sense. He could put his hand on any document he required within seconds.

'I meant,' he went on sourly, 'get on with the filing out in your office.'

With another pout, and a little wiggle of her

bottom for Seb's benefit, Bronwen flounced out of the office, closing the door behind her with unnecessary force.

Seb followed her progress with a smirk, but Truffler quickly brought him back to the matter in hand. 'You were saying about your dad having had this offer.'

The boy picked up his coffee and took a sip. 'It wasn't exactly an offer. More like . . . an investment opportunity.'

'And it come to him in the nick?'

'That's right.'

' 'Cause he's . . . what? . . . three years in now, is he?'

'Two and a half. Into a seven-year stretch. Mind you, with good behaviour and —'

'Yes, sure, sure.' Truffler nodded impatiently. 'So what was this "investment opportunity"?'

'Well,' said Seb in his best Captain of School accent, 'my father' like a lot of people in the nick, he suffers financially.'

'Right.'

'I mean, obviously he's got a bit stashed away . . . stuff that wasn't recovered from the last job. It's a tidy sum, but, you know, with inflation and what-have-you . . .' The boy shook his head gloomily, '. . . well, seven years on it's not going to be worth that much.'

'He hasn't got it on deposit or . . . ?'

Seb drew his lips tight across his teeth as he explained, 'Only in a manner of speaking. And you don't get much interest from a deposit that's six foot under Epping Forest.'

'Ah,' said Truffler, understanding. 'No. No, you don't.'

'Anyway,' the boy continued, 'the old man'll be pretty close to retirement, really, when he comes out . . . and he'll have lost a lot of his contacts, so even if he did want to get back into the business, he might find it tough . . . and, well, there's no way he's going to keep my mother in the style that she's become accustomed to on a state pension . . . so it's no surprise he was interested when he heard about this way of making his money work for him while he's inside.'

'Do you know the details of what it was, this investment plan?' asked Truffler urgently.

But Seb shook his head. 'No. I do know it involved Mum taking out a second mortgage on the house.'

'Oh?'

'Needed to raise fifty grand,' the boy explained. 'That's the stake.' Answering the alarm in Truffler's eyes, he went on, 'It's no problem. All be paid off again when dad gets out and reclaims the Epping Forest stash. And in the meantime that fifty grand will've doubled? Trebled? Who can say?'

Truffler looked sceptical. In his line of business he had come across too many investment opportunities guaranteed to double or treble the stake of the poor sucker who put his money into them. 'But you don't know what the actual investment was?' he asked. Seb shook his head. 'Or how Stan got to hear about it?'

The boy brightened. 'Oh yes. I do know that. It was through a bloke who was in the nick with the old man.'

'What was the bloke's name?'

'Blunt. Does that mean anything to you?'

'Oh yes,' said Truffler, slowly nodding his head. 'That certainly means something to me.'

Chapter Eighteen

Mrs Pargeter's wardrobe was both extensive and expensive. It very firmly reflected her character. Not for her were the muted fondant colours patronized by senior members of the British Royal Family. Not for her the subtle beiges and fawns which some women of ample proportions favour as a means to anonymity, to draw attention away from their bulk.

Mrs Pargeter had never attempted to hide her dimensions. She knew that such a task was hopeless, anyway, and that apparent success at it could only be self-delusion; but, apart from that, she had never felt the need to disguise her outline. Rather she gloried in it. Mrs Pargeter had always felt herself to be the right size for the person she was — and certainly the late Mr Pargeter had never had any complaints.

He had always been a lavish provider — and even, in some cases, purchaser — of clothes for his wife. He knew her style exactly, and on his varied travels would always be on the lookout for the bold silks and cottons that so flattered her generous curves.

Since his death, Mrs Pargeter had had to do all her own shopping, but so distinct was her sartorial identity that she never had any problems making decisions about what to buy. A dress or a suit was either right for her or wrong. Trousers and hats were never right for her. Nor were tights; Mrs Pargeter always wore silk stockings. Her underwear, even though her husband was no longer around to appreciate it, remained frivolously exotic. And the right shoes for Mrs Pargeter always had surprisingly high heels, which gave a pleasing tension to her well-turned calves and ankles.

She dressed carefully for the appointment she had made following her consultation of the Yellow Pages. And she dressed excitedly, rather relishing the idea of taking on another identity. It wasn't fancy dress, though; she wore her own clothes, but selected the brightest and most ostentatious to create a heightened version of her natural style. What she was after for the encounter to come was an ensemble which breathed too much money.

And she was happy that the effect had been achieved. She had asked Hedgeclipper Clinton — and Erasmus, it was impossible these days to have one without the other — to bring up her jewellery box from the hotel safe, and selected a matching set of ruby-and-diamond necklace, bracelet and cluster earrings. They were gems which had once belonged to a Cabinet minister's mistress, but the late Mr Pargeter had thought his wife a much more suitable proprietor and had arranged the transfer of ownership in his own inimitable way. Mrs Pargeter would under normal circumstances only have worn them in the evening, but their daytime brightness gave just the right over-the-top quality to the character she was proposing to play.

When she was dressed to her satisfaction, she did a little twirl for the benefit of the late Mr Pargeter's photograph on the bedside table. 'What do you think, love? Teetering on the edge of vulgarity — hm? Yes. Just about right, I'd say.'

She grinned and sat down on the bed. 'Now I'm going to be a good girl,' she continued to the photograph, 'and make sure that someone is aware of where I'm going, and what I'm going to do when I get there. I remember what you taught me, love — never take any unnecessary risks.'

She reached for the telephone.

In Truffler Mason's outer office Bronwen looked on admiringly as her boss ushered Seb out. Truffler shook an admonitory finger at the boy, saying, 'And remember, young man — in future you keep on the right side of the law.'

Seb grinned lazily. 'All right, all right. You sound like a blooming community policeman.' He beamed a roguish look at Bronwen and let a ripple run through his uncovered biceps. 'See you again I hope, gorgeous.'

The secretary gazed after him dreamily as he winked and went out through the door. 'Oh . . .' she sighed, her voice Welsher than ever in its wistfulness. 'What would I have to have to get one like that?'

'Plastic surgery?' her boss suggested mildly.

'Now listen, Truffler! Don't you —' But her fury was cut short by the telephone's ringing. She snatched up the new receiver as if prepared to do Grievous Bodily Harm to that one too. 'Hello, Mason de Vere Agency.' She looked across vindictively at Truffler. 'Yes, the bastard is here.' Standoffishly, she thrust the phone towards him. 'Mrs Pargeter.'

He grinned and moved towards his office. 'I'll take it through there.'

Mrs Pargeter found herself in the unusual situation of being embarrassed. Telling Truffler what she proposed to do had seemed easy when she thought of it. Now she was actually talking to him, she could anticipate all the kinds of objection he was likely to make. So she began with a little prevarication before moving on to the real subject of her call.

'Nothing more been heard from Fossilface O'Donahue, has it?' she fluted ingenuously.

'Not from my end, no. I should think he's gone to ground again. Why — Hedgeclipper hasn't had any more trouble, has he?'

'No, no. In fact, from Hedgeclipper's point of view, Fossilface has done him a favour. That bloody monkey. Hedgeclipper's just devoted to Erasmus — still walks round the hotel most of the time with the thing on his shoulder. They're inseparable.'

'Isn't that causing problems for him professionally? I mean, doesn't the average guest somewhere as swish as Greene's Hotel find it a bit odd that the manager is always accompanied by a marmoset?'

'Not at Greene's, no. Because the "average guest" here is an American with more money than sense, and they're "just thrilled" by what they regard as another heart-warming example of "lovable British eccentricity".'

'Ah. With you.' A silence. 'Was that what you were actually ringing about, Mrs Pargeter?'

'Well, erm . . . in a way,' she replied evasively, and moved into further delaying tactics. 'Maybe Fossilface has given up on his campaign of "restitooshun"?'

'I wouldn't be too sure of that,' said Truffler darkly. 'I've a feeling our charitable loose cannon's still out there, priming his powder for yet another hideously inappropriate gesture.'

'Oh dear.'

'You heard what he did to Keyhole Crabbe, did you?'

'Yes.'

'Bloody nasty, that could have been, if the screws in Bedford had found the stuff . . . Keyhole's always been so careful about his reputation. I mean, if word got around that he was the kind of geezer who leaves his professional equipment lying around in the nick . . . well, his image'd be well and truly scuppered.'

'You're right.'

'No, I think we should still be very much on the lookout for Fossilface's next attempt to demonstrate his sense of humour.'

'Yes, 'cause, of course, although he did Hedge-clipper over and tied him up, he still hasn't made his act of "restitooshun" there, has he?'

'No. And he hasn't paid his dues to Gary yet either. Or to Concrete Jacket. Or to me,' Truffler concluded gloomily. 'Don't forget I'm on his list too.'

'What kind of "restitooshun" do you reckon he's going to make to you? How did he do the dirty on you in the past? Because if you knew what kind of thing he was likely to come up with, you could be on your guard, couldn't you?'

'Huh. You make it sound easier than it actually is, Mrs Pargeter. A man could go mad trying to piece together the bizarre way a mind like Fossilface O'Donahue's works.'

'But you must know what wrong he did you . . . what offence he's likely to try and make "restitooshun" *for?*'

'Oh yes,' Truffler agreed mournfully. 'I know that all right. Fossilface got at my records — burnt a whole lot of them.'

'What kind of records?'

'I'd got some dirt on him and some of his mates. Pretty inflammatory stuff.'

Mrs Pargeter couldn't resist the joke. 'Probably that was why he found it so easy to burn.'

But Truffler was too resentfully deep in memories to respond to her humour. 'Irreplaceable, that material was. I'd built it up over years . . . just like your husband told me to. "Never hurts to have a bit of information on people you're working with," he always said to me. "You never know when it's going to come in handy".'

'What for?' asked Mrs Pargeter innocently.

'Well, when you're dealing with villains, it's good to have something against them. So you can put the screws on, come heavy with the blackmail or . . .' he seemed to sense disapproval creeping into the unseen eyes and quickly changed direction, '. . . or pass the information on to the police like a good citizen.'

'Yes. Yes, of course. Oh well, good luck, Truffler. Maybe by now Fossilface O'Donahue will have learnt how a sense of humour works, and make you some form of "restitooshun" that's actually appropriate.'

'Yes,' Truffler growled. 'And maybe Lord Lucan'll be the next prime minister.'

There was a silence. Mrs Pargeter knew she could no longer put off the real purpose of her call.

'Truffler, it's all *right,*' she found herself saying a few minutes later, soothing the predictable outburst detonated by the announcement of her plan.

'Well, I don't like it,' Truffler grumbled. 'You're taking an unnecessary risk.'

'I know what I'm doing. There's no way he could have a clue who I really am, anyway. The appointment's made in the name of Lady Entwistle.'

He didn't sound mollified. 'It's still a risk. Clickety Clark's a nasty piece of goods, and if he's got Blunt working with him too —'

'I'll be all right.'

'Hm.' Still not convinced. 'So . . . what's Lady Entwistle like?'

'Well, I was just deciding that. She's a widow, definitely, and her husband left her *very* well provided for.'

'Typecasting?' Truffler suggested.

Mrs Pargeter was affronted by the idea. 'Oh no. Lady Entwistle's got more money than sense. Keeps complaining she doesn't know what to do with the stuff.'

'Sounds a perfect mark for an unscrupulous conman . . .'

'Exactly. That's the aim of the exercise. Lady Entwistle is a real sitting duck. Much younger than her late husband, needless to say. Oh no, she was a bimbo before the word was invented. And she's dead common.' A smile crept over Mrs Pargeter's generous features as she came up with the perfect background detail. 'Yes,' she said, 'her husband got knighted in Harold Wilson's Resignation Honours List, that's it.'

Truffler chuckled. 'Well, you just be careful. Bloke you're up against may have a veneer of civilization, but deep down he's a real nasty mean villain.'

'Don't worry,' said Mrs Pargeter. 'I've dealt with a good few of them in my time.'

Chapter Nineteen

The foyer of Greene's Hotel was a miracle of understated elegance. An eighteenth-century French chandelier spread beneficent light over antique oak furniture and delicate glassware. As Mrs Pargeter came out of the lift into this paradigm of grace, Hedgeclipper Clinton was emerging from his office with a piece of paper and a puzzled expression. On his shoulder, Erasmus chattered excitedly. 'Now what on earth can this mean?' said the manager, almost to himself.

'Problem?' asked Mrs Pargeter.

'Well, I don't really know. I've just received this rather bizarre fax . . .'

He held the sheet across to her. There was no originating address or fax number, but across the top was a logo of a circular smiley face. Beneath this were the words: INSTAQUIP — THE PERFECT JOKE FOR EVERY OCCASION.

'Oh dear,' said Mrs Pargeter, thinking back to her recent conversation with Truffler Mason. 'Oh dear.'

'What's up?'

'Well, I'm not sure, but . . . just let me read it.'

With foreboding, her eyes reverted to the page.

'How many lightbulbs does it take to change a man?' she read.

Her mind framed yet another 'Oh dear' as she discovered the answer. 'It depends whether the power's on or not.'

There seemed little doubt about the fax's provenance. The telltale signs were all there — a joke, or rather the structure of a joke, clearly the work of someone to whom jokes did not come instinctively. In fact, it read like an early effort of a student whose first language was not humour.

'Hedgeclipper,' Mrs Pargeter said gently, 'you remember Fossilface O'Donahue?'

The memory was so strong that the manager didn't even notice her use of his forbidden nickname. 'I'm hardly likely to forget him in a hurry, am I? You don't on the whole forget people who burst into your office, overpower you and tie you up, do you?'

'No. I gather you and he worked together some time back . . . when you both were involved in business dealings with my husband?'

'I wouldn't say we "worked together". We saw each other from time to time, but our relationship was not close. In fact, we hated the sight of each other. That bastard Fossilface bloody nearly got me killed, you know.'

'Really? How was that?'

'The fact is, Mrs Pargeter, that back in those days I had a nickname. Hedgeclipper. I think you're probably aware of it.' Mrs Pargeter graciously inclined her head. 'Yes, well, the fact is

140

that I had that nickname for a reason. When I was working for your late husband, I often used to use hedgeclippers to . . . erm . . .' He seemed to be having difficulty in finishing his sentence.

Mrs Pargeter helped him out. 'To prune hedges and that kind of thing?'

'And that kind of thing, yes,' he agreed, though in a manner that suggested his point had not been entirely clarified.

'I remember,' Mrs Pargeter went on, 'you once come out and did all the front privet at our big house in Chigwell, didn't you?'

'Yes, when I was lying low after that job in Tooting Bec and —'

'When you were having a well-earned rest,' Mrs Pargeter corrected him smoothly.

'Yes. Yes, of course.' Hedgeclipper Clinton grimaced, once again having difficulty in coming up with the right formula of words. 'Erm, well, what happened was . . . on one occasion I was about to set out on a job for your husband, which was going to involve my using the hedgeclippers in . . . er, a less horticultural context. The fact is, Mrs Pargeter, that though your husband had a lifelong abhorrence of violence . . .'

'Oh certainly,' the wide-eyed widow confirmed. 'He was the gentlest of men. Would never knowingly have hurt a fly.'

'No, exactly. Not *knowingly*. And he always had remarkable control over precisely what he did and didn't know, I found.'

'Yes.'

'I mean, on this occasion I'm talking about, I was going out with my hedgeclippers to . . . well, not to beat about the bush —'

'To *prune* the bush, perhaps?' Mrs Pargeter suggested meekly.

'Not that either, in fact. No, I was to be there, with my hedgeclippers, to, as it were, prune the aspirations of our opponents. They were a some-what ungentlemanly band of jewel thieves, and I was to be present at the encounter . . . to make them see things your late husband's way . . . and — though of course I didn't make a habit of such behaviour — I was even prepared to use violence if it became necessary . . .'

'Though I'm sure that was one part of the arrangement my husband didn't know about.'

'No, I have no doubt he was very careful *not* to know about that part of the arrangement. Any-way, from the point of view of our side, my pres-ence was very important. Our opponents were known to be armed with baseball bats, and there's nothing so dispiriting to the malicious wielder of a baseball bat than to have it cut off at the handle by a judiciously manoeuvred set of hedgeclip-pers.'

'Yes.' Mrs Pargeter was thoughtful for a mo-ment. 'They must have been very powerful hedgeclippers you were using. I mean, cutting through the handle of a baseball bat is rather different from snipping off an unruly twig of privet.'

'That is certainly true, Mrs Pargeter. Erm, perhaps what we have here is a problem of nomenclature. I was nicknamed "Hedgeclipper" because I did start my career by using exclusively hedgeclippers. The fact is that, by the stage in my career that we're talking about, I had enlarged my repertoire of equipment. And though I still refer to the instrument as "hedgeclippers", by then what I was actually using was . . . a chainsaw.'

'Oh.'

'A rather powerful, large, petrol-driven chainsaw . . .'

'Ah.'

'And it was my chainsaw that Fossilface O'Donahue sabotaged.'

'Oh dear. How did he do it?'

'Unbeknownst to me, he had emptied the petrol tank. With the unfortunate result that, when the tone of our meeting started to sour and, seeing eight men armed with baseball bats advancing on me, I pulled the ripcord to start my hedgeclippers . . .'

'. . . or chainsaw . . .'

'Or chainsaw, yes . . . nothing happened. Well, perhaps it would be more accurate to say what did happen was not what I had planned to happen . . . or indeed wished to happen.' He winced with recollected pain. 'Not one of the happiest days of my life, Mrs Pargeter.'

'No, I can believe it. So,' she continued, piecing the scenario together, 'the wrong that Fossilface O'Donahue did you concerns fuel, or power?'

'Yes,' Hedgeclipper Clinton concurred.

At which moment, the chandelier went out, and the distant hum of office machinery suddenly stopped.

Hedgeclipper Clinton, Erasmus still gibbering on his shoulder, held the antique candlestick aloft as he led Mrs Pargeter down into the hotel's cellar. He had been in favour of just calling one of his maintenance staff to investigate the power failure, but she had insisted that they do it themselves. She was wary of the processes of Fossilface O' Donahue's 'restitooshun'.

The cellar covered the entire floor area of the hotel, and was divided into sections by upright concrete pillars. Only the nearest of these could be seen, however, because the space in between had been filled high with what, in the uncertain flickering of the candle's light, appeared to be metal blocks.

'What the hell are those?' Hedgeclipper Clinton murmured, moving closer to inspect them.

Mrs Pargeter had already got the answer from the smell rising from a spillage on the floor before Hedgeclipper's candle illuminated the confirmatory sign on the side of one of the cans: PETRO-LEUM SPIRIT.

The cellar was full of cans of petrol. In front of the ranks of them were two gleaming new emergency generators. On one was stuck a note, headed by the same smiley-face logo that had been on the fax.

The message read: NOW YOU'LL NEVER BE POWERLESS AGAIN — AS THE BISHOP SAID TO THE ACTOR.

Incomprehensible as ever. Yes, there was no doubt they were once again up against Fossilface O'Donahue's slowly developing sense of humour.

Hedgeclipper Clinton chuckled. 'Well, going to be a long time before I have to queue up at the petrol pumps again. It looks as if I haven't come out of this "restitooshun" business so badly.'

'Don't be too sure, Hedge—'

But Mrs Pargeter didn't get the chance to finish her sentence. At that moment, Erasmus, bored by not being the centre of attention, had grabbed the lighted candle from his owner's hand and leapt down on to the cellar floor.

He waved the candlestick around frenziedly. Its light was reflected in the rainbow spill of petrol as the flame swirled ever closer.

'Come on, Erasmus . . .' Hedgeclipper Clinton cooed. 'Come on . . .'

The hotel manager was down on his knees, inching closer to the marmoset. His pinstriped trousers were already sodden with petrol. The pool of fuel on the floor was spreading; one of the containers must have been holed.

Mrs Pargeter looked anxiously at the wall of petrol cans. Neither she nor Hedgeclipper had voiced it, but it didn't take a lot of imagination to work out what would happen if the petrol ignited. Goodbye, Mrs Pargeter. Goodbye,

Hedgeclipper Clinton.

And, come to that, goodbye Greene's Hotel, along with any residents who had the misfortune to be inside at that particular moment.

Goodbye, Erasmus, too — though Mrs Pargeter reckoned that was one bereavement she could bear with equanimity, even enthusiasm. Not, of course, that she'd be in much of a position to enjoy the benefit of his departure.

The marmoset seemed fully aware of what was at stake, and was enjoying himself hugely. There was no longer any problem about who was the centre of attention. Erasmus waved the candle flame lower and lower as his owner drew closer.

Oh dear, thought Mrs Pargeter, as an unpleasant new recollection invaded her mind. She wasn't very knowledgeable about science, but even she knew the basic principles of the internal combustion engine. It wasn't the petrol itself that ignited; it was the vapour. And in an enclosed space that vapour would quickly build up to become extremely flammable. Oh dear.

What a way to go, Mrs Pargeter thought with deep resentment. Killed by the combined efforts of a monkey and a criminal idiot trying to teach himself how to have a sense of humour. No, any death but that. It would be just too humiliating.

As she had the thought, Hedgeclipper Clinton suddenly launched himself forward to make a grab for Erasmus. The marmoset, anticipating his move, leapt up into the air and grabbed the handle of one of the highest cans. Hedgeclipper skidded and fell face down in the oil slick. The candle flame flickered with the movement, but quickly re-established its steady glow.

Erasmus and Mrs Pargeter both were aware of the sound at the same moment. It was a steady dripping. The feeble candlelight caught the sheen of individual droplets as they fell free from the can next to the one from which Erasmus was swinging.

There must have been some kamikaze training in the marmoset's background. Mrs Pargeter would have sworn she saw glee in his eye as the monkey slowly changed the angle of the candlestick to bring its flame closer to the leak.

It was time for desperate measures. Mrs Pargeter let out a sudden shriek, a high-pitched imitation of a monkey s cry. Maybe she had captured the admonitory note of Erasmus's mother when angry; maybe the marmoset was simply distracted by the sound. For whatever reason, he turned suddenly towards her.

Mrs Pargeter leapt forward and blew the candle out.

'You know,' she said to Hedgeclipper, as they climbed wearily out of the cellar after he had restored the electrical supply, 'I think we may have to go out and get Fossilface O'Donahue before he does anything else.'

'Yes,' the hotel manager agreed. 'If we can find him.' He turned his head round to the marmoset by his ear. 'You know, Erasmus,' he said in play-

147

ful reproof, 'sometimes you're a rather naughty little monkey.'

Which, in Mrs Pargeter's view, was something of an understatement.

Chapter Twenty

The photographic studio, in a discreet Mayfair town house, had a slightly dated feel to it. The artfully scattered chaos gave the impression that its owner had never really recovered from seeing *Blow Up* back in the sixties (which in fact he hadn't).

Nor was this idea dispelled by the appearance and manner of the studio's presiding genius. Clickety Clark looked like a gnarled relic of the Summer of Love. He was in his late fifties, a fact accentuated rather than disguised by his youthful dress. The battered Levis, the denim shirt strained over prominent belly and the leather blouson had a perversely ageing effect, compounded by the ponytail into which his thinning grey hair was straggled back.

And Clickety Clark's professional style suggested that he'd watched too many documentaries about the early David Bailey (which in fact he had). He moved continuously round the room in a gait midway between a dart and a lumber, constantly framing images in the little viewfinder he carried on a leather thong around his neck. And all the time, in a deliberately roughened street-credible voice, he kept mumbling instructions to his assistant, Abbie.

She was a pretty dark-haired girl in her early twenties. Clickety Clark's manner to her suggested she was a necessary and appropriate accessory to his image as photographic genius. Her manner to him was tolerant and obedient, but the wry light in her eye made it clear she had no illusions at all about her employer. Abbie was the kind of girl who could recognize bullshit when she saw it, and on her first meeting with Clickety Clark had had no difficulty in identifying cartloads of the stuff.

The subject of the morning's shoot, Mrs Pargeter — or to give the name by which she had introduced herself, Lady Entwistle — was seated on a manorial oaken throne against tastefully draped red velvet curtains. At a table by her side was a vase of bright peonies. Mrs Pargeter knew that the vivid fabrics she had so carefully selected that morning clashed hideously with this background, but she made no demur. It was in character for Lady Entwistle not to notice — or more probably to approve — such a wince-inducing concatenation of colours.

Clickety Clark crouched rather unsteadily on the floor and peered up through a camera lens at his subject. 'Don't worry, Lady Entwistle,' he said in his phoney laid-back accent. 'I can really make you look wonderful.'

Lady Entwistle smiled graciously. 'Oh. Very nice. Thank you so much, Mr Clark.'

He lifted a magnanimous hand towards her. 'Please . . . call me Clix.'

Mrs Pargeter saw Abbie's shapely brows rise heavenwards at this, and had to restrain herself from making eye contact with the girl. While to do so would be very in character for Mrs Pargeter, Lady Entwistle was definitely a person who lacked the capacity for irony.

So she just said, 'Thank you . . . Clix then.'

The genius snapped a finger. 'More light on the drapes, Abbie.' Obedient, quick and skilful, the girl made good the deficiency. 'This portrait going to be a present for your husband then, is it, Lady Entwistle?' 'Clix' asked. Another snap of the fingers. 'Higher up, Abbie.'

His sitter assumed a face of pious mourning. 'Ah, no. Regrettably, Sir Godfrey is no longer with me.' In reply to Clickety Clark's quizzical look, she amplified this, lest Sir Godfrey might mistakenly be thought to have been bimboed away. 'He has gone to a better place.'

'Oh. Oh dear.'

Enjoying her fabrication perhaps a little too much, Mrs Pargeter could not resist embroidering further. 'He lost his life tragically in a yachting accident off Mustique, where we were staying with some rather eminent friends . . . whose names I'd perhaps better not mention. The wind changed suddenly and the boom of the yacht caught him on the temple. It was touch-and-go for seven weeks.'

'I am sorry.'

'But eventually it turned out to be go.'

'How sad.' Clickety Clark waved dismissively

to his assistant. 'Spilling at the top a bit, Abbie.'

'This was a few years back,' Lady Entwistle went on. 'I have managed, after a considerable struggle, to come to terms with my grief.'

'Oh, good.'

'And, fortunately, Clix,' the lady confided, warming to her theme, 'Sir Godfrey did leave me extremely well provided for.'

This information definitely registered with Clickety Clark, but all he said was, 'Well, that's nice, isn't it? Pull that curtain across to the right now, Abbie — want a bit more spread. Husband left you a nice house and all that, did he, Lady Entwistle?' he asked casually.

'Very nice indeed. All of the houses are. As it happens, though, the main residence is a little old-fashioned for my personal taste, so I'm having a new home built that's more suitable — more *me* if you know what I mean . . .'

'Oh, really?'

'Trouble is, the building work is currently in a state of suspension, no progress at all.'

'Why's that then, Lady Entwistle? Contractor gone bankrupt? That's the usual reason these days.'

'Oh no. If only the situation were that simple. No, you're hardly going to believe this, Clix — but the builder who's doing the job has just been arrested for murder.'

'Good heavens.'

'Gentleman called Mr Jacket . . .'

The name struck home, but Clickety Clark

152

tried to hide his involuntary reaction in sudden movement. Splaying his hands wide, he snapped, 'More than that, Abbie! Spread the drapes out more!'

Mrs Pargeter was determined not to leave the subject there. 'Maybe you've seen about his arrest in the papers?' she hazarded.

But Clickety Clark was quickly back in control of himself. 'Maybe. Yes, rings a distant bell,' he said, before moving the subject deftly on. 'The way I operate with portraits, Lady Entwistle, is I take a lot of exposures, and then you and I go through the contacts and we decide which one we're going to work on.'

'Work on?'

'Oh yes.' He smiled with a confidence verging on smugness. 'As a photographer, you see, my skills tend to be in the, er, post-production phase.'

'Oh?'

For a moment he looked suspicious. 'I'm surprised you didn't know. You said the Marchioness of Didsbury recommended me to you.'

Mrs Pargeter had hastily to remind herself of her background lies. 'Oh yes, of course. She did mention your special skills, yes.'

'Turn the flowers a bit to the left, Abbie,' the genius said with an imperious flick of his hand, and then turned back to his sitter. 'Lady Entwistle, you must've seen the portrait I did of the Marchioness. Knocked a good fifteen years off of her. Not a wrinkle in sight. Ironed out those bags under her eyes like they'd never been there. And I can do the same for you, no problem.'

She couldn't get out of her natural character quickly enough to stop the instinctive reaction. 'Actually, I'm quite attached to some of my wrinkles.'

Clickety Clark chuckled. 'Well, you point out the ones you like, and I'll get rid of all the others, eh?' Lady Entwistle vouchsafed his pleasantry a smile, so he continued, 'I don't come as expensive as plastic surgery, you know.'

'No. You don't exactly come cheap, though, do you . . . Clix?'

He opened his hands out in a gesture of helplessness. 'If I came cheap, my clients wouldn't think they was getting their money's worth. The sort of clients I deal with, that is.'

'Of course they wouldn't,' said Lady Entwistle reassuringly.

'Still . . .' the genius smiled a wolfish smile, '. . . doesn't sound as if the financial side would be a problem to you, Lady Entwistle.'

She let out a tinkling laugh. 'Oh no. Good heavens, no.' Then her brow furrowed. 'It's sometimes quite difficult, though, in these dreadful times, to know what to do with one's money . . .'

He was instantly alert. 'Oh yes?'

Lady Entwistle made a gesture of hopelessness. 'Well, a lot of the traditional investment areas — you know, Lloyds, Barings, that kind of thing — have become so unreliable, it's hard to know where to turn.'

'You find that, do you, Lady Entwistle . . . ?' asked Clickety Clark with a little too much diffidence.

Mrs Pargeter pressed on blithely. 'Yes. Goodness, I'd be delighted to hear of some different kind of investment opportunity.'

'Really?' The photographer was thoughtful for a moment, then cast a critical look at his sitter's backdrop. He shook his head. 'Something still not right with this set-up. Abbie, could you bring up that big plantstand from the basement? Yeah, and bring us an aspidistra to put on it.'

The girl nodded and set off on her mission. The minute she was out of the room, Clickety Clark moved closer to Mrs Pargeter's throne. 'Lady Entwistle, when you said you was looking for a different kind of investment opportunity . . .'

Chapter Twenty-One

Clickety Clark ushered his sitter fulsomely out on to the pavement of the discreet Mayfair square. As he did so, Gary's limousine, which had been cruising round the block to avoid a shoal of predatory traffic wardens, slid smoothly up towards them.

'Don't worry, Lady Entwistle,' the photographer oozed, 'I'll be in touch as soon as I've got a set of contacts I'm happy with. Then we can go through them and decide where my magic can be worked to best effect, eh?'

'Well, I'm not after too much magic, Clix,' she giggled coyly. 'Don't want to run the risk of people not being able to recognize it's me.'

'No danger of that at all. It'll definitely be you, but a you that looks as good as you possibly can. And everyone who comes to your house will be able to see a photograph of someone looking their absolute best.'

'What, you mean — and compare it unfavourably with the original?'

'No, no.' The photographer came in quickly to soothe her, but stopped when he caught the twinkle in her eye.

'Only joking, Clix.'

'Ah. Yes. Right.'

'Well, I'll wait to hear from you.' Mrs Pargeter stepped towards the limousine. Clickety Clark moved forward to open the back door for her.

'Yes, Lady Entwistle, fine.' He moved his head closer to hers as she was about to get inside. 'And, with regard to the other matter . . . the, er, "investment opportunity", I'll have to make a few enquiries, but hopefully, by the time we meet up to look at the contacts, I'll be able to fill you in a bit more on that.'

'You couldn't fill me in a little bit more now, could you?' she asked hopefully. 'Just tell me what sort of area of investment we're talking about?'

The photographer shook his head. 'At the appropriate time,' he said with a wink.

Mrs Pargeter resigned herself to not getting more information at that stage. She wasn't too upset. Her Lady Entwistle act had definitely engaged Clickety Clark's interest in her as a potential investor. He was hooked.

She got into the limousine and he closed the door after her. 'Right you are,' she said imperiously.

The uniformed chauffeur put the vehicle into gear. 'Very good, milady,' said Gary, who, needless to say, was in on the deception.

Lady Entwistle gave the photographer a regal wave as the limousine slid forward. Her last view of Clickety Clark was of a lined face almost bisected by a sycophantic smile.

The minute she was out of sight, however, the smile dropped sharply from his lips and a hard shrewd light came into his eye. Mrs Pargeter was too far away to see him nod to the driver of a parked blue Jaguar on the other side of the road.

The man's dark glasses turned up from the paper he was pretending to read, and he caught the photographer's eye. Clickety Clark gave a little jerk of his head towards the departing limousine. The driver nodded and started the engine. His car began to follow Gary's.

Mrs Pargeter was unsuspicious of surveillance, so she did not look round to see who was driving the Jaguar a few cars behind. She probably wouldn't have recognized the man in his dark glasses, anyway.

Had he taken them off, though, she might have been able to identify a face she had seen twice — once in a photograph on Truffler Mason's desk, and once on the screen of Ricky Van Hoeg's computer.

The man was Blunt.

Chapter Twenty-Two

Truffler Mason's car was like an extension of his clothes. Indeed, if any automobile manufacturer had tried to design a vehicle which breathed the image of tired sports jacket, crumpled beige trousers and black Gas Board Inspector shoes, they would undoubtedly have come up with a dented brown Maxi. As a symbol of the post-war decline of the British motor industry, the car had about it an air of failure, which exactly matched Truffler's own aura of defeatism.

In fact, of course, the detective was considerably more positive and cheerful than he appeared. At that detail the comparison between man and car ceased. The Maxi did not possess a secret, more attractive, persona.

It was four o'clock in the morning. The Maxi was parked in a dark lay-by on a country road a few miles out of Bedford. The meagre moonlight outlined two figures in the front. Truffler sat in the driving seat. Beside him was Keyhole Crabbe. Both held plastic cups. Truffler's contained coffee; Keyhole was just replenishing his with whisky. He proffered the half-bottle towards the detective.

'Sure you won't?'

Truffler shook his large head decisively. 'No,

no. Driving. Wouldn't do any good for me to get stopped — particularly with you on board.'

'No.'

'Wouldn't do you a lot of good either, come to that. What with you being kind of "absent without leave", as it were.'

'True.'

The detective took a thoughtful sip of coffee before continuing his debriefing. 'So you reckon there's a lot of them in the same position?' he asked eventually.

'Certainly four in my nick. I've been asking around. And, by coincidence — or possibly not by coincidence — they're all blokes who've got a stash hidden away somewhere.'

'And all blokes who've been offered some "investment opportunity" while they're inside?'

'Right. And in each case it was Blunt who made the offer.'

'Yes . . .' Truffler nodded ruminatively. 'He's on a permanent tour of Her Majesty's prisons, old Blunt, isn't he? Short stretches here, there and everywhere.'

'Hm.'

'But I really can't cast him in the part of the geezer who thought up the scam — if it is a scam. He hasn't got the braincells for that kind of work. He's just muscle. Got to be someone else behind him.'

'Right. 'Course, the other thing all these blokes I've talked to in the nick have in common is that in each case their wife or girlfriend or whoever's managed to raise fifty grand for their stake.'

'But none of them'll tell you what the money's for?'

'No. I've tried all my favourite methods of winkling it out — usually very effective they are too — but this time no dice. It's all very secret . . . like they was almost embarrassed about it.'

Truffler grimaced ruefully. 'The perfect con.'

'Howdja mean?'

'One of the many wise things the late Mr Pargeter told me was that the best cons're always the ones where the people who've got conned are too ashamed to own up to what they done.' Keyhole Crabbe nodded agreement to this truism, as Truffler Mason went on, 'Anything else your four got in common?'

The prisoner thought about his answer for a moment. 'Just that they're all in for longish stretches. None be out for another three years, anyway.'

Truffler rubbed his chin. The rasp of bristles was unnaturally loud in the silent car. 'I wonder . . .'

A new recollection came to Keyhole. 'One other thing too . . .'

'What's that?'

'Couple of them mentioned that their old ladies've been abroad while they been inside.'

Truffler was instantly alert. 'What, off with boyfriends you reckon? Doing naughties? Having it off with randy geezers who're lining themselves up for broken legs — or worse — when the husbands get out?'

Keyhole Crabbe quickly dampened such tabloid speculation. 'No, no. Nothing like that. No Roger the Lodgers involved. The husbands knew all about these trips, seemed pleased about them even.'

'But surely . . .'

The prisoner opened his hands wide in apology. 'All I got, Truffler. Not another dickie bird. Sorry. I'll go on probing, of course, but, like I say, they keep clamming up on me.'

'Hm.' Truffler knew his informant too well to push for more. If Keyhole Crabbe said that was all he'd got, then that was all he'd got. 'Well, can't thank you enough. Mrs Pargeter'll be really grateful to you.'

'Least I could do for her,' Keyhole shrugged.

'I'll follow up through my contacts in a few other nicks,' said Truffler. 'See if it's happening anywhere else.' He turned the key in the ignition, and the Maxi shuddered into asthmatic, apathetic life. 'Right then, Keyhole . . . better get you back inside, eh?'

'Yeah.'

The car moved tentatively out of the lay-by in the direction of Bedford Prison. After a moment of silence, Keyhole Crabbe said, 'On the other hand . . .'

'What's that?'

'Think perhaps I should pay a call on the old lady.'

'Oh, right.'

'If it's not out your way . . . not holding you up?'

'No problem.'

'It's not for me, you understand,' Keyhole confided, 'but Mrs Crabbe . . . well, she does like her conjugal visits.'

'Sure.'

'So, Truffler, if you can take me back to the old domestic nest, and then if you don't mind hanging about and having a cup of tea . . .'

'No problem. I'll be happy to sit around for an hour or so.'

'Hour or so?' an appalled Keyhole Crabbe echoed. 'Give us a break, Truffler. Ten minutes'll be fine.'

Truffler Mason had driven straight on from Bedford, and arrived in time to join Mrs Pargeter for the Greene's Hotel 'Full English Breakfast'. They both ordered everything, and she insisted they should wait till the toast and marmalade stage before talking business.

After Truffler had brought her up to date with Keyhole Crabbe's investigations, Mrs Pargeter poured some more coffee for both of them, and sat back thoughtfully. 'If it is a con . . . presumably whoever's taking the money is going to be well away before all the lags who've paid up come out of prison.'

'I'd have thought so,' Truffler agreed. 'Why else would Blunt only have targeted the ones doing longish stretches?'

She drummed her fingers on the table. 'I wonder what it is he's been offering them?'

'And on whose behalf he's been offering it?'

'Yes. Maybe Lady Entwistle'll hear something more from Clickety Clark, though I'm not sure she will. I'd've expected someone like that to be quicker off the mark in his follow-up . . .'

Truffler Mason shook his head with foreboding. 'I still wish you hadn't done that, Mrs P.'

'What?'

'The false identity, Lady Entwistle routine. Clickety Clark's quite a canny operator. I've a nasty feeling you may've put him on his guard by doing that.'

'Nonsense,' said Mrs Pargeter breezily. 'He didn't suspect a thing.'

Truffler was not convinced. 'Well, I hope you're right.'

' 'Course I am. And I know what we're going to have to do next — go straight to the source, talk to Blunt. That's the only way we're going to find out anything. He's not inside at the moment, is he?'

'No. For once, he's actually at large. Which must make quite a change for him. As we found out from Ricky Van Hoeg, our man's been in and out like a yo-yo last couple of years.'

'All different prisons, weren't they?'

'Oh, yes.'

'And all short sentences?'

'That's right.' The detective caught something in his employer's tone and looked at her shrewdly.

'What're you suggesting?'

'Just that his sequence of sentences might have been a deliberate policy. Sort of sales trip, you could say . . .'

'Hadn't thought of that, Mrs P., but it makes good sense.'

'Also the fact that he's not inside now might mean things're coming to a head.'

'How do you mean?'

'Sales trips successfully completed — Blunt and his mates have creamed off all the loot they reckon they're going to get — next thing they'll do is make off with it.'

'You could be right.'

'Which makes it all the more urgent that we find Blunt before they leave the country.'

'Yes,' Truffler agreed grimly. 'I got some leads. Contacts I can check up on through my filing system. Or I can get more details from Ricky Van Hoeg if I need them. He can put out one of his requests for info on the Internet. Don't you worry, Mrs Pargeter, I'll track Blunt down for you.'

'Good. The next thing we must do is —'

She was stopped in mid-sentence by the appearance in the dining room of an obsequious Hedgeclipper Clinton. In his hand was a mobile phone. The only detail that once again let down his elegant image was the marmoset on his shoulder.

'Mrs Pargeter,' the hotel manager rippled subserviently, 'I'm so sorry to interrupt your breakfast, but there's a lady on the telephone asking for you. I wouldn't normally have butted in . . .' He put his hand discreetly over the receiver and breathed, '. . . but she does sound very distressed.'

'Thank you,' said Mrs Pargeter, taking the phone. 'Hello? Tammy?'

An expression of horror transformed her normally benign features. 'What! Don't worry, we'll be there straight away!'

Chapter Twenty-Three

The discordant decorative styles of the Jackets' home somehow made the devastation even more shocking. The multicoloured windows had been smashed; wallcoverings of hessian, flock and vinyl had been slashed; the panelling and extensive range of doors had been splintered by sledgehammer blows. The artex ceilings and swirly carpets had been sprayed with unspeakable fluids. The floor was a Dresden of contorted wrought-iron, shattered onyx and the shards of glass figurines.

Tammy Jacket's personal decor — on this occasion an electric blue angora sweater, silver leather miniskirt, tartan tights and gold pixie boots — was in perfect order, but she looked at least as devastated as her house. She stood in the fractured doorway to her beloved sitting room, her sobbing only quietened by the reassurance of Mrs Pargeter's plump arm around her waist. Truffler Mason picked his way delicately through the debris on the sitting-room floor.

'It's so awful,' Tammy murmured. 'All our lovely things.'

Mrs Pargeter was far too tactful to question the description. Instead, she stroked soothingly as she said, 'Yes, I know. But at least thank goodness you weren't here.'

'No, but the next time I might be. I can't . . .' The thought was too much, and the intensity of Tammy's sobbing once again increased.

'It's all right, love,' Mrs Pargeter murmured. 'You'll be all right. Truffler . . .' she called into the sitting room.

He turned round at her summons and raised a lugubrious eyebrow. 'Yes?'

'I'm going to take Tammy away. Take her somewhere safe.'

He nodded. 'Good idea. I'll have a nose round here for a bit.'

As the rhythm of Tammy's sobbing became more even, Mrs Pargeter once again looked around the bomb site that had been a sitting room. 'Do you reckon it was just random destruction, Truffler? Or someone giving Tammy some kind of warning?'

He shook his head. 'No. I think they was definitely looking for something.' He turned to Tammy with surprising gentleness. 'That list you give me . . . you reckon it was everything?'

She sniffed to regain control of herself. 'Everything valuable, yes. I mean, everything Concrete and I would consider to be valuable.'

It crossed Mrs Pargeter's mind that these two definitions might not in everyone's mind coincide, but she suppressed the disloyal thought.

Tammy Jacket shook her shoulders purposefully. 'I must go and repair my make-up. Then we'll be off, will we, Mrs P.?'

'Yes. Off somewhere safe, where you won't

have to worry about a thing.'

'Great.' Tammy paused at the foot of the stairs. 'Bless you,' she said before she disappeared. 'Both of you.'

Mrs Pargeter moved closer to Truffler and surveyed the devastation. 'Blunt, do you reckon?'

The detective nodded decisively. 'Has all the hallmarks of his subtlety, yes. I'd put money on it.'

'Hm. Makes it all the more important we find him . . . before he does any more harm.'

'Don't worry. We'll get him. Soon as I'm back in the office, I'll go through my files. I'll track him down all right, and see he's stopped from doing any more mischief.'

Mrs Pargeter was intrigued to know how this outcome would be achieved, but restrained her curiosity. She had never forgotten the late Mr Pargeter's advice about there being certain subjects of which she did not need ever to have any knowledge.

'Meanwhile,' said Truffler, looking again at the wreck of the Jackets' sitting room, 'I'll go through this lot with the proverbial fine toothcomb. Get back to you when I find out what it was they was after.'

'*When?* You're that confident?'

'Yes, Mrs P. I am that confident. These bastards came here to get something, and I'm going to find out what it was.'

Gary's limousine eased along the road like an

electric iron over linen. 'Nearly home now,' the chauffeur called out to the two women in the back. 'Won't be long.'

Tammy Jacket was seized by another moment of panic. 'But suppose they find me there?'

Mrs Pargeter's comforting arm was instantly around her shoulders. 'Nobody's going to find you at Gary's place. You'll be fine.'

Tammy let out a little whimper. 'Oh, but what can Concrete have done, for them to have smashed our place up like that?'

'Don't worry. I know Concrete. I'm sure he hasn't done anything really bad. And we'll get to the bottom of it. Truffler's good, he'll sort things out. And it's not as if we just got Truffler on our team. There's a whole lot of other people who used to work with my husband and every one of them's more than ready to —'

She was interrupted by the trilling of the earphone. Gary answered, and switched it through to the back. 'Pick up the handset, Mrs P. It's Truffler.'

'Hello?' said Mrs Pargeter into the receiver. 'You getting anywhere?'

'Think so. Been through all the safes Tammy listed for me — and blimey, there was a lot of them. Concrete designed that house with more hiding places than a conjuror's tailcoat. But, so far as I can tell, nothing in any of the safes has been touched.'

'So all the really valuable stuff's OK? They haven't got any of it?' said Mrs Pargeter, raising her voice to include Tammy Jacket in this good news.

Tammy managed a half-smile through her tears.

'That's the way it looks, yes,' Truffler confirmed. 'Only thing I haven't been able to find, though . . .'

'Is what?' Mrs Pargeter prompted.

'. . . but I can't really think why it would be valuable to anyone . . .'

'For heaven's sake, Truffler! What're you talking about?'

'Well, it was what Tammy was showing us when we was round her place the other —'

'*What!*' Mrs Pargeter almost screamed in exasperation.

'It was that brochure thing. Those photos of that property development Concrete worked on in Brazil.'

'Oh?'

'Now why on earth would those be of value to a bunch of villains?' asked Truffler.

'Why indeed?' Mrs Pargeter wondered.

Chapter Twenty-Four

Gary's cottage looked as if it was auditioning. Auditioning maybe for the lid of a chocolate box, or Conservative Party election literature, or for one of those British Tourist Board publications which are left optimistically around American travel agents and hotels.

The thatch was done to a turn like the top of a perfect cottage loaf. The black beams, wary of right angles, veered appropriately from the symmetrical. Between them, the walls were as pristine white as Mrs Pargeter's conscience or Gary's criminal record. The leaded windows were suitably irregular. Here were no double-glazed sheets overlaid with fancy beading; the panes' bulges and concavities bore witness to their authentic individuality. The red-brick garden path undulated charmingly.

And, yes, around the green-painted wooden door, roses bloomed.

The sun shone. The requisite birds swooped and glided. Fluffy clouds gambolled like lambkins across the clean blue pasture of the sky, and a warm breeze stirred the lethargy of the rose bushes.

There was even a smell of newly baked bread in the air.

Whatever show it was auditioning for, the cottage must surely have got the part.

Gary's limousine was parked on the gravel in front of the garden, and through the high open gates of the adjacent thatched barn, which he used as a garage, the gleaming bonnets of the rest of his fleet of hire cars could be seen.

Behind the cottage, in a garden heavy with nodding hollyhocks, three women gathered on wooden chairs round a rustic table. The neat evenness of the grass was a tribute to the efforts of Gary and his little red cultivator/tractor, parked neatly under an apple tree. A trailer full of garden refuse was attached to the machine, but somehow even that contrived to look neat.

Mrs Pargeter gazed with satisfaction over the vista of farmers' fields beyond the neatly trimmed hedge, while Denise, Gary's pretty blonde wife, ministered to Tammy Jacket with tea and fancy cakes.

Gary himself was at the end of the garden, wielding a petrol-powered strimmer, whose lethal circular blade attachment scythed through a patch of rough grass at the edge of the fields. The whirring of each burst from its motor alternated with the drowsy hum of insects. Gary worked systematically through the weeds, exuding the quiet contentment of ownership.

Mrs Pargeter extracted herself from a reverie of a rather pleasantly erotic country walk that she and the late Mr Pargeter had once taken in Oxfordshire, and concentrated on what Denise was saying. '. . . and Gary's a bit old-fashioned about the idea of my working. He feels that a husband should be able to support his wife and family on his own.'

'Well, that's fine, isn't it?' Mrs Pargeter agreed easily. 'Everyone doesn't have to be a feminist career girl, do they? Work out what suits you best as a couple, eh?' Denise nodded. 'And the car-hire business is going awfully well, I gather?'

'Oh yes. Splendidly. Has Gary had a word with you about it yet, Mrs Pargeter?'

'About what?'

Denise looked a little confused, as if she had spoken out of turn. 'Oh, nothing. No, the business is going very well indeed. We're getting more and more weddings and stuff . . . seems to sort of spread by word of mouth.'

'Provide a good service and people'll come back for more. My husband always used to say that. Certainly worked for him.'

'Yes. Did you ever have a job yourself, Mrs Pargeter? I mean, while your husband was alive?'

Mrs Pargeter smiled enigmatically. 'Erm. Not a job as such, no.' She looked fondly across at Tammy Jacket, who was demolishing a cream cake with considerable enthusiasm. 'You feeling better now, love, are you?'

Not a hair of the copper-coloured coiffure was stirred by the vigorous nod of reply. 'Yes. Yes, thank you. Much more relaxed.'

'Good.'

But the smile faded quickly from Tammy's face. 'I am worried about Concrete, though . . .'

Mrs Pargeter tried to reassure her. 'Come on, you weren't before. You said you knew he'd get off and there was no problem.'

'Yeah . . .' Tammy's mouth twisted with uncertainty. 'But when I visited him yesterday, he was all . . . odd.'

'Howdja mean — "odd"?'

'Well, like sort of . . . scared. I never really seen Concrete scared before.'

'Any idea what he was scared of?'

'Well, it was almost like he was . . . scared of being in the nick.'

'Oh? I thought he was quite used to . . .'

The words were out before Mrs Pargeter had time to stop them. But fortunately Tammy Jacket was too preoccupied to notice any potential lapse of decorum.

'Yes, yes, he is. It's odd, though, Mrs Pargeter. It's like there's something he's afraid of the other lags finding out . . .'

'But you've no idea what it could be?'

Slowly, Tammy Jacket shook her head.

Mrs Pargeter pressed on in the hope of further illumination. 'Do you think it's possibly something to do with Willie Cass's death?'

There was a bewildered shrug. 'I suppose it could be, but I don't know what.'

'You say Concrete didn't know Willie that well?'

'No. Well, I mean just like you do know somebody you work with . . .'

'Hm.'

Tammy was silent and thoughtful for a moment. Then she said slowly, 'Unless of course they got pally when they was out in Brazil together.'

Mrs Pargeter focused sharply on the woman. 'Willie Cass was in Brazil with Concrete?'

'Yes. Didn't I say?' The casualness of her reply showed how unaware Tammy was of the information's significance.

'No,' said Mrs Pargeter, just managing to keep the edge of annoyance out of her voice. 'You didn't.'

Denise was sensitive to the slight change in atmosphere. Instantly she proffered the pot. 'More tea, anyone?'

A little time had elapsed. The tea things had been cleared from the table, and Denise was inside the cottage doing her chores. Gary was still down the garden. His strimmer was switched off now. He was tidying up, raking together the last swathes of fallen grass, and dumping them in the trailer of his cultivator.

Tammy Jacket lay in a hammock, with a magazine propped up in front of her. But the long gaps between page-turnings and the frequency with which the magazine slipped down on to her lap suggested sleep was not far away. Finally, after the shock of what had happened to her house, she was beginning to relax.

Mrs Pargeter looked up and smiled as Gary came towards her. 'A good job jobbed?' she asked.

'Yes.' The chauffeur grinned slightly awkwardly, and lingered in front of her as if there was something he was trying to say.

'Problem? Something worrying you?'

'Well, no. Not as such. Not exactly a problem, Mrs P. Just something we once talked about.'

'Mm?' Mrs Pargeter was pretty certain she knew what was coming. Denise's earlier hesitancy had forewarned her. She saw the chauffeur twisting his fingers nervously. 'Oh, for heaven's sake, Gary. You don't have to be shy with me. If there's something you want to say, say it.'

'Yes, well, erm . . . the thing is . . . I don't know if you remember, but a little while ago we were discussing me getting an older car for, erm . . .'

Mrs Pargeter couldn't be doing with all this hesitancy. 'A vintage Rolls-Royce for weddings, yes.'

'And I, um . . .'

'You've changed your mind about accepting my offer of a loan for you to buy one.'

'Well, yes, I . . . The thing is . . . Denise said —'

'Have you seen one you like?'

An uncontrollable smile spread over Gary's features. 'There's a beauty advertised locally. 1938. I've had a butcher's at it. Done a test-drive, and all. In lovely nick. Not cheap, mind, but —'

'Great. Go out and buy it.'

'I mean, obviously, if you only mentioned the idea of a loan in a rash moment, I wouldn't want —'

'Of course I didn't mention it in a rash moment.' Mrs Pargeter took a chequebook out of her handbag. 'How much do you want?'

'Now, Mrs Pargeter, it's important that we both regard this as a business arrangement and —'

'Gary,' said Mrs Pargeter, in a tone as near to exasperation as her equable nature ever got, '*how much do you want?*'

Chapter Twenty-Five

In its infinitely graceful British way, the summer afternoon was giving way to evening. Shadows had lengthened. An ecstatic Gary was away confirming the purchase of his beloved 1938 Rolls-Royce. Tammy Jacket still breathed deeply and easily in the hammock. From inside the cottage wafted smells of some wonderful evening meal Denise was preparing.

Mrs Pargeter, still seated at the rustic table, was talking on a mobile phone to Nigel Merriman. She brought the solicitor up to date with what Tammy Jacket had told her. 'At least it gives us another line of enquiry,' she said. 'It becomes increasingly important to find out what Concrete Jacket was doing in Brazil, doesn't it?'

'I have already questioned my client on this matter, but I am afraid he was as unforthcoming about that as he has been about everything else.'

'Yes, but at that stage you didn't know Willie Cass was out there with him, did you?'

'I'm not sure that's going to make a lot of difference.'

'No, but still worth trying, isn't it?'

'Everything is worth trying, Mrs Pargeter, if it offers even the smallest possibility of clearing my client. I will certainly raise the matter again when

I am next in touch with him.'

'Excellent. Meanwhile, it gives me another line to pursue.'

'Yes.' There was a tentative silence. 'Might I ask, Mrs Pargeter, how exactly you will be conducting your enquiries?'

She chuckled. 'Better not. My late husband was always a great believer in keeping a bit of mystery about one. Let's just say I've got some very useful helpers, and don't worry — you and I are on the same side, Mr Merriman. We're both going to do our level best to see that Concrete Jacket walks out of that prison without a stain on his character.' She corrected herself. 'Well, without any *more* stains on his character, anyway.'

Nigel Merriman acknowledged this with a rather prim little laugh. 'Yes, of course. And, Mrs Pargeter, I trust I can rely on you to let me know as soon as there's anything else to tell my client?'

'Of course you can.'

'Thank you so much. I may say it is a great comfort for me to know that I have your support in this distressing affair.'

'No problem at all.'

'When one works in the legal profession, cynicism about the concept of justice does, I'm afraid, become an occupational hazard.'

'Don't you worry about that, Nigel my love. We'll see to it that Concrete Jacket gets . . .' She paused, trying to think of the right words.

'Justice?' the solicitor prompted.

'What he deserves, I think'd be nearer the

mark.' Mrs Pargeter chortled. 'And if that happens to be justice too . . . well, there's a bonus, isn't there?'

'Yes. Thank you so much. Goodbye.'

'Goodbye.' Mrs Pargeter switched off the phone, pushed in its aerial, and tiptoed across to the hammock. The depth of her sleep had ironed away the wrinkles of anxiety, giving Tammy Jacket's face an almost childlike innocence.

'Don't you worry, love,' Mrs Pargeter murmured. 'We'll soon have Concrete back for you.'

Tammy Jacket had finally woken up and gone off to have a shower before dinner. Gary had not yet returned. 'No doubt off joyriding in his new motor,' said Denise fondly. 'Really appreciate you lending him the money for it, Mrs Pargeter.'

'Don't even think about it. Anyway, what we're talking about here is a business proposition. I'm now an investor in your family business. And I'm pretty shrewd about my investments. I wouldn't have lent him the money if I didn't see a profit for me in it.'

'Well, thanks all the same. Gary'll work hard, don't you worry.'

'I know that. I have total confidence in him. You expecting him back for dinner?'

'Oh yes. Always back when he says he's going to be.' Denise coloured, almost embarrassed by her devotion. 'He's a good husband to me, Gary is.'

'Good lad all round,' Mrs Pargeter concurred.

Denise grinned with pride. 'Now let me get you a drink. Vodka Campari was it Gary said you liked?'

Mrs Pargeter did not deny that that would be very acceptable. She stayed in the garden, her eyes half-closed, feeling the last rays of the day's sun wash over her.

When Denise reappeared with the vodka Campari, she was also holding the mobile phone. 'Call for you, Mrs Pargeter. A Mr Mason.'

The phone was handed over, and Denise went discreetly back to her cooking.

'Truffler . . . How's it going?'

'Hasn't been great,' the Eeyore-like voice intoned. 'Been following up a few leads on finding out where Blunt might be. No dice, though.'

'You been on to Ricky Van Hoeg?'

'Mm, just leaving there now. He's put requests for info on the Internet, but hasn't got any response so far.'

'Well, we do know where Clickety Clark is — or at least where he has his base. At the worst, you could get the information out of him.'

'Yes, I'm sure I could, but I don't want them put on their guard — not more than they are already. Don't worry, Mrs Pargeter, once I get back to the office, I'll have it sorted in no time. I'm on my way there right now.'

'Couldn't you have phoned Bronwen and got her to give you the information?'

'No, I couldn't. For two reasons, as it happens. One — she doesn't know her way around my filing system. I'm the only person in the world who knows the way around my filing system.'

Remembering the scattered debris of paper in the office, Mrs Pargeter had no difficulty in believing the truth of this.

'And two — Bronwen wasn't in the office today.'

'Oh?'

'Had to be in court.'

Mrs Pargeter's response was instinctive. 'What's she done?'

'No, no, she hasn't done anything. It's to do with the divorce.'

'Oh, right. Yes, of course.'

'Which means not only won't I have had any work from her today, but if I stay in the office I won't get any work from her tomorrow either — just a lot of vitriol on the subject of the poor unfortunate who was her most recent husband.'

'Oh dear.'

'Which is why I'm going to the office to check my files *now*. At least I'll be able to work uninterrupted.'

'Yes, of course. Well, good luck.'

'Don't worry. I'll've got an address for Blunt by the end of the evening. If I track him down before eleven, I'll let you know. Otherwise talk in the morning, eh? Cheerio, Mrs P.'

Truffler Mason parked the Maxi outside the betting shop and reached in his pocket for the keys to his office. He lurched wearily up the narrow stairs, past the defunct travel agents on the first floor, and put his key into the lock of the shabby door that read: MASON DE VERE DETECTIVE AGENCY.

The moment he switched on the light, he saw the full extent of the transformation. Bronwen's outer office, previously a jungle of buffs and browns, now gleamed in pale greys and charcoals. It looked like an advertisement for an office equipment company.

Her battered desk had been replaced by a minimalist glass-topped number, on which coyly perched a state-of-the-art computer, sentried by phone and answering machine. On new shelves behind the desk demurely sat a virgin photocopier, fax and printer.

The only object that remained from the office's previous incarnation was the wall-planner for the current year. There were still no stickers on it for CURRENT COMMITMENTS, but whereas previously its newness had put the rest of the room to shame, against all the pristine equipment it now looked tarnished and apologetic.

Of the piles of paper and folders that had once cluttered the space, there was no sign.

It only took two strides of Truffler's long legs to cross the outer office. With a sense of imminent disaster, he grasped the handle and swung the door open. He flicked the lightswitch on.

His room looked even more like something from an office-furniture catalogue than Bronwen's had. The massive black leather swivel chair could have been cut up to make a three-piece suite, with enough left over for a set of matching luggage; the desk was king-size; and the computer on it looked capable of every human activity short of making babies — though, given the speed of current technological change, quite possibly it could do that too.

Of the files, the folders, the shoeboxes full of history, the documentary fragments that represented the most exhaustive criminal archive outside the FBI, not a scrap remained.

Full of foreboding, Truffler Mason crossed to the desk. On its gleaming surface was a sheet of paper.

He groaned at the sight of the smiley face that headed it. Underneath was written:

Q: HOW CAN YOU TELL WHEN AN IRISH-MAN'S BEEN USING YOUR COMPUTER?
A: BY THE MARKS OF CORRECTING FLUID ON THE SCREEN.

Underneath the joke was written:

I'VE CHUCKED OUT ALL YOUR OLD FILING SYSTEM AND REPLACED IT WITH THIS STATE-OF-THE-ART KIT. SORRY ABOUT THE WRONG WHAT I DONE YOU IN THE PAST AND . . . WELCOME TO THE TWENTY-FIRST CEN-TURY.

It wasn't signed, but then it didn't need to be.

The style of 'restitooshun' was all too painfully recognizable.

'Oh, Fossilface . . .' Truffler groaned. 'Have you any idea what you've done?'

Chapter Twenty-Six

'Well, it is encouraging in one way,' said Mrs Pargeter soothingly.

'What way?' Truffler Mason's voice growled from the other end of the phone.

'With regard to his sense of humour. I mean, that Irish joke — OK, it's as old as the hills, and it wasn't very funny in the first place, but the fact remains that it *is* a joke. It has the structure of a joke; he's actually got things the right way round this time.'

'Mrs Pargeter, I don't care if he's won the Nobel Prize for Joke Construction — what Fossilface O'Donahue has done is to destroy over twenty years of patient research. Those files of mine are entirely irreplaceable. He's, like, destroyed the whole basis of my business. He's obliterated information that Scotland Yard could only dream of possessing.'

'I don't suppose it's possible . . .' Mrs Pargeter suggested, '. . . that Fossilface has actually had all your data transferred on to the new computer system he's installed. I mean, if that's happened, then he really will have done you a favour, won't he?'

'Oh yes.' Truffler's voice was heavy with sarcasm. 'Wouldn't that be wonderful? And likely too, when you're dealing with a Fairy Godmother as warped as Fossilface O'Donahue! No, that was one of the first things I checked. The only actual data that's been keyed into the computer goes as follows: "I say, I say, I say. Have you heard the one about the Lunchpack of Notre Dame?" "No, I haven't. How does it go?" "What's wrapped in cellophane and swings from a steeple?" "I don't know. What *is* wrapped in cellophane and swings from a steeple?" "It's the Lunchpack of Notre Dame!!!" '

'Oh dear,' said Mrs Pargeter. 'Clearly getting that Irish one right was just a fluke. Fossilface hasn't really caught on to the principles of joke-telling at all, has he?'

'No, he hasn't. All he's caught on to is the only thing he was ever any good at — totally destroying people's lives.'

'But at least now he's doing it from the best of motives. He really is trying to make "resti-tooshun" for the evil he's done in the past.'

'Quite honestly, Mrs P., I'd rather have the original Fossilface than a Fossilface on the side of the angels. At least in the old days you could predict the kind of vindictive mayhem he was likely to unleash. His charity is much more threat-ening.'

'Mm. You're right.' There was a silence before, very gingerly, Mrs Pargeter moved the subject on. 'So, Truffler, you can't follow up the investigation the way you were hoping to?'

'No.'

'So what's going to be your next line of approach?'

'Well, I'm rather limited for choices now, aren't I? I'll go and talk to Rita Gertler.'

A puzzled 'Mm?'

Truffler explained. 'Seb's Mum. You know, old Stan the Orang-Utan's wife.'

'Oh, right.'

'Maybe get a lead there.' But, even by Truffler's dour standards, he didn't sound hopeful. With an effort, he forced a more positive note into his voice. 'Don't you worry, Mrs Pargeter. Only a minor setback. I'll find Blunt for you. He can't be far away.'

Neither of them could possibly know how accurate Truffler Mason's words were. Blunt was at that moment less than fifty metres away from Mrs Pargeter. He was sitting in his Jaguar under the shadow of some trees, keeping surveillance on Gary's cottage.

It was one of those summer nights which would never get properly dark. Blunt detected movement and shook himself out of the reptilian doze in which he normally conducted surveillance operations. He could lie for hours like a crocodile, immobile with half-closed eyes, apparently unaware and unthreatening. But when something happened, he would be instantly awake. And, like the crocodile, instantly ready to wreak havoc.

The front door of the cottage opened and his quarry, resplendent in a cream négligé, emerged into the front garden. The moonlight shone on the silk, lending a ghostly outline to Mrs Pargeter's ample curves.

Blunt waited to see what would happen next. Clickety Clark had said they should try to snatch her if they got the chance, but Blunt was always wary of acting on his own initiative. A suggestion from Clix wasn't the same as an order from higher up. And would they want just Mrs Pargeter on her own? Wouldn't they want him to bring the Jacket woman as well? Blunt didn't want to make a rash move that might get him into trouble later on.

On the other hand, it would be nice to get a pat on the back for pulling off something good . . . And, after all, she was just one elderly lady on her own. No problems about overpowering her, trussing her up in the back of the Jaguar and delivering the spoils back to London. Mrs Pargeter was getting uncomfortably close to the truth; soon she might — perhaps she already did — know the details of the scam in which Blunt and Clickety Clark were involved. Having come this far, so near to getting away with it, so near to dividing up all that lovely money, they didn't want their careful planning scuppered by one little old lady.

There was also an element of grudge-settling . . . The late Mr Pargeter and Blunt hadn't parted on the happiest of terms, and indeed the longest of Blunt's many prison sentences would never have happened but for the intervention into a police investigation of Mrs Pargeter's husband.

No, there were scores to be settled, all right. Blunt didn't reckon Clickety Clark would make a fuss if their quarry was delivered a little 'roughed up' . . . The idea caught hold; his breathing grew heavier. It'd been a long time since he'd really let himself go, a long time since he'd justified his name — 'Blunt' as in 'Blunt Instrument'. Yes, maybe he should just —

His deliberations were interrupted by the sweep of powerful headlights turning a corner towards the cottage. Blunt shrank back into his seat, eyes once again in crocodile mode, as a splendid silver-gray vintage Rolls-Royce came to rest outside the garden gate. The woman in the cream négligé moved forward to greet the driver.

'Wondered where you were,' Blunt heard Mrs Pargeter's voice say. 'Denise was beginning to get a bit worried about you.'

'Sorry. Got carried away. Just had to take her out again after supper. She's such a beauty, I can't stop driving her,' said the chauffeur's voice.

'Glad you're pleased with it — her.'

'Pleased? That's an understatement. Step inside, Mrs P. Just have a look at her.'

Mrs Pargeter did as she was bidden, and when the passenger door closed, Blunt could hear no more of their conversation. His eyelids lowered even further, till they were only a paper's breadth apart. But he remained vigilant.

Inside the car, Mrs Pargeter was properly appreciative of all the features lovingly detailed by

Gary. She nodded approvingly at the polished chestnut dashboard, the array of gleaming metal instruments, the leather plushness of the upholstery. It had clearly been a good buy.

'I can't thank you enough,' Gary kept saying.

'Oh, for heaven's sake. It was a business loan. An investment. I firmly intend to make money out of my stake in your company.'

'Don't worry, you will, Mrs Pargeter. I guarantee you will.' Gary caressed the steering wheel lovingly. 'Fancy a quick spin, do you?'

'Well . . .' She was tempted. 'What about Denise, though? Won't she mind? Won't she want to come too?'

'No worries. She'll be asleep by now. Come on, just a quick circuit of the lanes.'

'OK.' Mrs Pargeter sat back luxuriously as the powerful engine took command.

The ride was as smooth as a dream of flying. Very relaxing. Mrs Pargeter knew that she would sleep even better than usual that night. (Not that she ever actually had trouble sleeping. At ease with herself, Mrs Pargeter's nights were always as sleek as the sheen on her silk stockings.)

Only as they drew up once more outside the cottage, while Gary was deliberating whether to leave the Roller outside or lock it up for the night, did a troubling thought enter Mrs Pargeter's mind. 'Gary,' she said, 'you remember Fossilface O'Donahue, don't you?'

'Of course.'

'And you know that he's embarked on this orgy

of misguided charity, bringing "restitooshun" to everyone he's wronged in the past?'

'Yeah, I heard a bit about that.'

'Well, I've suddenly remembered that your name was on the list of people he wanted to make "restitooshun" to.'

'Oh. Right. I'll be on the lookout.'

'So I was wondering . . . what wrong did he do you in the past? I mean, if we know the area in which he might be trying to make it up to you, perhaps we'll have a chance of stopping him from messing anything else up.'

'Good thinking. All right, well . . . Fossilface O'Donahue done the dirty on me in connection with a matter of transport. Bound to be, wasn't it?'

'Oh yes, I remember you mentioned something. About a getaway car. He didn't drain the petrol tank, did he?' asked Mrs Pargeter, thinking of what had happened to Hedgeclipper Clinton.

'No, no, it was different from that. Quite as destructive, mind you. What Fossilface done was, he put nails in the tyres . . . not so's to puncture them straight away, but so's the nails'd work themselves in once you was up and running. I was up and running fast — doing ninety in the outside lane of the M1 — when the first tyre went. Dead hairy, swirling round like Torvill and Dean I was, nearly lost control. Tell you, Mrs P., if your husband hadn't insisted on me doing that skid-pan training before he let me work for him,

I'd've been a goner. He was a really caring employer, you know, Mr Pargeter was. Thought of everything.'

'True,' his widow replied distractedly. She was too concerned with thoughts of Fossilface O'Donahue to take much notice of yet another compliment. 'Hm, so knowing the way Fossilface's mind works — or trying to get into the perverse workings of Fossilface's mind — maybe we should be on the lookout for some kind of "restitooshun" involving tyres?'

'Any idea what?'

Mrs Pargeter shrugged. 'If I had the skills to predict that, I'd win the National Lottery every week.'

'Right.' Gary yawned. 'I'm for bed. It's a mild night. Maybe I will leave the Roller out for —'

'I'd lock it up if I were you,' said Mrs Pargeter firmly. 'I'm not having my investment put at risk.'

She went back to the cottage and bed. Gary drove the Rolls-Royce into the converted barn, and locked the large doors front and back. Then he too went to bed.

Neither Mrs Pargeter nor Gary knew that all their actions were still being watched.

Chapter Twenty-Seven

The next stage of Truffler Mason's enquiries, forced on him by the loss of his archives, brought him up against that common British phenomenon, middle-class upward mobility. In all their researches into tribes from Poluostrov Tajmyr to Papua New Guinea, anthropologists have yet to discover a less secure social grouping than the British middle class. The status of this section of society is always fluid. They cannot find stasis, as the aristocracy and the genuine working class frequently do. The middle classes are never able to forget where they've come from, and spend all their time in heart-searching assessment of the number of degrees by which they are on the way up or down from that starting point.

The dilemma was well expressed by the household in which Truffler Mason found himself. Stan Gertler — known professionally as Stan the Orang-Utan, for reasons which you will either understand instinctively or which you don't need to know about — was definitely born 'lower middle class'. In fact, the young Stan might have slipped back quite comfortably into the working class, but for an aspiring mother who was determined to make something of her husband and her child. For there is nothing more daunting in the world than an aspiring mother with middle-class ambitions.

Stan Gertler's social instability was then aggravated by his own marriage. Rita, with whom he fell in love as suddenly and heavily as he habitually knocked over night watchmen, regarded herself as 'middle class' — though she would more accurately have been described as 'upper lower middle class' — and, needless to say, her only ambition was to become 'upper middle class'.

To this end, she moved her husband away from his Stoke Newington roots to the nice genteel suburb of Muswell Hill, and never did anything so lower-class as to ask him where his money came from but instead proceeded to spend a great deal of it on stripped pine, spice racks and Laura Ashley curtains.

When their son was born, she branded him for life with the hopefully classy name of Sebastian, and tried to use him as a crampon to pull the family further up the sheer cliffs of middle-class fulfilment. This involved sending the boy to a public school to develop both his vowels and his inbuilt antennae for the recognition and avoidance of anything 'common'.

It had been Mrs Gertler's hope that in time her son would meet a nice girl from the 'upper upper middle class' — or even, dare one hope it, 'the aristocracy' — to produce a new generation of children who, instinctively and without prompting, would for the rest of their days treat au pairs and waiters like dirt.

But her fond aspirations did not look likely to be realized. Sebastian was a sad disappointment to his mother. Even his expensive vowels had become deliberately roughened by that inverted snobbery to which public school boys are so prone. And his taste in women was proving to be decidedly down the tacky — not to say 'rough trade' — end of the market.

Thank goodness Rita Gertler didn't know that her son was currently spending his days menacing motorists with a squeegee, thought Truffler Mason as she dispensed dry sherry and gave him a guided tour of her taste in interior decor.

'Of course,' she was saying, in an accent that still remained more broken glass than cut glass, 'the sideboard's Regency.'

'Of course.' Truffler looked appraisingly at the item in question. 'Very nice, Rita. Stan always did have a wonderful eye for antiques, didn't he?'

'Oh, I'll say.'

'Knew how to pick them. Knew what he wanted, and didn't bother with any of the other stuff.'

'That's so true.'

'Wherever he went in, he always knew what to take and what to leave.'

Rita cleared her throat, indicating that the boundary of some middle-class prohibition was being approached a little too closely. Then she moved on. 'I like to think Sebastian's inherited some of his father's flair.'

Sebastian, incarcerated for his mother's benefit

in a tweed sports jacket, checked shirt and paisley tie, smiled weakly.

'Oh, what?' asked Truffler. 'You mean flair for —'

Rita came in firmly to divert the direction of the conversation. 'Flair for spotting antiques. Sebastian's doing a Fine Art course at university . . . aren't you, Sebastian?'

'Yes, Mummy,' he replied, uncomfortably back in his best public school accent.

'Very nice.' Truffler looked blandly across at the young man. 'That all he's doing at the moment then, is it?'

Sebastian eased an awkward finger round the inside of his collar, as his mother said, 'Oh yes. In three years' time he'll have a degree. That's how universities work, you know.'

'Really? I'd often wondered.' She was unaware of his irony, as Truffler went on, 'So his dad'll just be out for the ceremony, won't he?'

Rita pursed her lips, leaving Truffler in no doubt that his remark had not been in the best of taste. He hastened to cover over the gaffe. 'Keeping well, is he . . . Stan?'

'Very well, thank you.'

The response was rather curt, but she softened when Truffler continued, 'And you're looking very good yourself.'

Slightly preening, she simpered back, 'How kind. Anno Domini marches on, but one . . . endeavours to do one's best.'

' 'Course.' He slid the conversation seamlessly

into the next stage of his investigation. 'Look like you've caught the sun too, Rita. That all been in this country, has it?'

'Oh yes. Just here, sitting out on the patio.' She pronounced the word to rhyme with 'ratio'.

'Ah, right. So you haven't been abroad since . . .' there was a conscious effort of tact, '. . . since Stan's been away?'

'Well . . .' Rita confided, 'I did have one rather enjoyable little trip . . .'

'Really?' Truffler's response was casually poised, as if the subject held only the mildest of interest for him.

'It was what I believe is vulgarly known as a "freebie" . . .'

'Nice.' Then, as if his enquiry arose out of mere politeness, he asked, 'Long way away, was it?'

'Yes, it was, actually, Truffler. Rather an exotic location, as it happens . . .'

'This all sounds very mysterious, Rita.'

She gave a coy flutter of the eyelashes, attracted to the idea of being a woman of mystery. 'Well . . .'

'Perhaps you'd like to tell me about it?' Truffler suggested.

He and Sebastian leant forward together, as Rita Gertler prepared to tell all.

Chapter Twenty-Eight

That morning Gary's cottage remained in audition mode. When viewed from the other side of the road, a slight haze of mist still blurred the cottage's outline, but that seemed only to make the archetypal scene more beautiful (or it would have done to a watcher with more aesthetic sensitivity than Blunt). And the mist was of the kind that would soon be burnt away by the midday heat of another perfect summer day.

This was good news for the bride and groom in whose honour Gary was tying white satin ribbon across the bonnet of his new Rolls-Royce. Their special day, which would be immortalized in endless photographs — and probably a video — was going to be a perfect English summer day. If the marriage subsequently went wrong — and of course one in three marriages do — at least they wouldn't be able to blame the weather.

The doors of the barn adjacent to the cottage were open. The building had double doors front and back; from the front the vehicles would drive out proudly on their various missions; while the back led to a yard where necessary maintenance was carried out. On the gravel drive Gary, neat in his uniform, seemed almost umbilically attached to his precious Rolls-Royce. Two other drivers, equally smart, adjusted white satin bows and buffed the already glasslike bonnets of two lesser limousines. The wedding was a good booking for the company.

Gary's wife Denise came out of the cottage, dressed in a smart turquoise suit and white hat. It was her friend who was getting married. Gary had also been invited as a guest, but preferred to be present in his professional capacity.

'Look great, love,' he said to Denise, as she approached the car. 'I'd marry you any day.'

'Well, forget it,' she said tartly. 'I'm already married.'

'Damn, always a snag, isn't there?' Gary gave his wife an affectionate peck on the cheek. 'Better be off then, had we?'

She looked at her watch. 'Mm. Don't want to make the bride more nervous than she already will be.'

'OK.' With elaborate ceremony, he opened the back door of the Rolls-Royce and ushered his wife inside. He turned and waved to the two chauffeurs behind. 'Time to hit the road, fellers.'

The elegant convoy of gleaming cars eased effortlessly off the gravel and on their way. Their departure was noted with approval by the two men sitting in the parked Jaguar under the trees on the other side of the road

'Off to his wedding booking . . .' said Clickety Clark, who had arrived secretly in the middle of the night.

Blunt grunted.

'. . . leaving Mrs Pargeter and Tammy Jacket on their own,' the photographer continued gleefully.

Blunt grunted again.

'Shall we move in then?'

A third grunt, then Blunt turned the key in the ignition. The Jaguar was about to leap forward, when Clickety Clark held up a cautionary hand. 'Hang about.'

Driving along the road towards the cottage was a battered old brown Maxi. They watched it park on the gravel, and saw the tall man who uncoiled himself from the driver's seat.

'Truffler Bloody Mason,' Clickety Clark murmured.

'He still wonky?' asked Blunt.

'No. Bloody gone straight, hasn't he? Private detective set-up he's got now. Mason De Vere he calls himself. Works a lot with Mrs Pargeter, I've heard.'

Blunt watched the tall figure stoop under the low doorway as he was let into the cottage. 'Shall we go and nail him too while we got the chance?'

The photographer shook his head. 'No. Don't want to take on three if we can avoid it. Give them half an hour. If he's not out by then, we'll think again.'

Blunt gave a curt nod and switched off the engine.

Unaware of the continuing surveillance of the cottage, Mrs Pargeter and Truffler sat at the rustic table in the back garden. Tammy Jacket was once again lying in the hammock, and once again fast asleep. The previous evening Mrs Pargeter had provided a couple of sleeping pills to relax her. Tammy had got up that morning for breakfast, but as soon as she lay down in the hammock, sleep had reasserted its control. Good thing too, thought Mrs Pargeter. More sleep she gets the better. Wash away all those nasty memories of what'd happened to her house.

'Never too early for a nice glass of Chardonnay,' Mrs Pargeter announced, as she poured out two, for herself and Truffler.

'I'd go along with that,' he replied mournfully, and took a grateful sip. 'Mm, that's good.'

She looked at him expectantly. 'So?'

'It was Brazil Rita went to,' Truffler confirmed.

'Good.' Mrs Pargeter's eyes glowed with the satisfaction of a correct conjecture. 'So it's got to be tied up with what I told you about Willie Cass.'

'Yes. What happened was . . . Seb's mum was offered an all-expenses trip out there. She wasn't the only one neither. I've checked with some other lags' wives. They got the same deal.'

'So what was the deal?'

'Viewing trip. To see the show villa.'

'The one Concrete built? Or rather the one Concrete and Willie built?'

'That's right.'

Mrs Pargeter chuckled. 'So it was like break time-share marketing? A party of lags' wives sent off to Brazil to check out the amenities?'

'That sort of idea, yes. Except it wasn't a party of them. Each one went out on her own. Got the guided tour of the show villa and was then offered a very good deal on one of the other villas on the estate.'

Mrs Pargeter nodded to herself as she thought it through. 'You can see the attraction, can't you? Safe, secure place. No questions asked about where the money came from. Ideal retirement location for . . . people in their position.'

'Exactly.' Truffler Mason warmed to his theme. 'The potential purchasers were very carefully targeted. All of them villains getting near retirement age. All with quite a bit of money stashed away, but money they might have had difficulty investing in the . . . er, more traditional manner.'

'I'm with you.'

Truffler elaborated further. 'Blunt'd keep his ear to the ground when he was inside until he found someone suitable. He'd sound them out, get them interested, and then Clickety Clark'd come in to do the sales pitch to the wives.'

'And do you reckon that's all he did?' Mrs Pargeter asked thoughtfully.

'Well, I'd assumed that . . .' But the look on her face told Truffler she had another idea. 'What're you thinking?'

Mrs Pargeter pieced it together as she went along. 'Listen. The wives were taken out to Brazil individually . . .'

'Right.'

'And we know that Concrete himself only built one villa . . .'

'But we've seen the photograph of the completed estate,' Truffler objected.

'A photograph,' Mrs Pargeter explained patiently, 'which someone so wanted not to be seen that they smashed up the Jackets' house to find it.'

Truffler stroked his chin while he took in the implications of this.

'I wouldn't have thought,' Mrs Pargeter went on, given his skills in post-production work, that doctoring a photograph like that would have presented Clickety Clark with too much of a problem . . .'

'Got you!' Truffler Mason snapped his fingers. 'You think all the lags have laid out money on the same villa? The rest of the estate doesn't exist?'

She nodded excitedly. 'That's the way I see it, Truffler, yes. Brazil's a long way away — unlikely anyone's going out there to check. The wives've all seen a lovely dream house — they're happy. The husbands think they've made a secure investment for their future — they're happy. And not one of the poor blighters realizes that they've all bought the same house. It's the perfect con. None of the victims're going to be out of the nick for another three years . . . and by then I care to bet that Clickety Clark and Blunt — and the money — will somehow've disappeared.'

Truffler nodded along with the explanation,

until he saw a snag. 'But then why did they frame Concrete? What'd they got to gain from that?'

'Concrete knew too much. So did Willie Cass. Willie was the bigger risk, because he was a real blabbermouth when he'd had a few drinks — so they topped him and then made the set-up look like Concrete'd done it. Old two-birds-with-one-stone syndrome.'

'But if Concrete's in prison,' said Truffler, 'then surely there's a danger he's going to meet the very people who've been conned out of their money?'

'Oh yes.' The violet-blue eyes shone as Mrs Pargeter saw everything falling into place. 'But do you think he'd tell them he was involved? No way. Oh no, the villains knew full well Concrete'd keep his mouth shut. Even trying to defend himself against the murder rap could've got him into deep water with the people who'd been conned. Truffler, it seems to me we now have the perfect explanation for Concrete Jacket's unwillingness to talk.'

'Do you think he was actually in on the con then?'

Mrs Pargeter shook her head firmly. 'I'd say he went to Brazil in good faith and did the building because they made him a good offer. Then he found out what was really going on and realized they'd got him.'

Truffler Mason grunted agreement, and rose urgently to his feet. 'Right. I got contacts in South America. First thing I'm going to do is check out this estate with the one villa on it.'

She looked up at him. 'And the second thing you're going to do . . . ?'

'The second thing I'm going to do,' said Truffler grimly, 'is I'm going to find Clickety Clark and Blunt before they make any more trouble.'

Had he realized how close his quarries were, Truffler Mason could have saved himself a lot of trouble. He could also have averted a lot of trouble for Mrs Pargeter and Tammy Jacket.

Sadly, however, in the excitement of having cracked the logic of the case, he did not demonstrate his customary vigilance. He was not aware how easily Clickety Clark and Blunt had penetrated the Lady Entwistle presence; nor did he know how closely the two villains had been following Mrs Pargeter's trail.

So, preoccupied with his own plans, Truffler Mason came straight out of the cottage, got straight into the Maxi, and drove straight off without a glance across the road to where a Jaguar lurked in the leafy shadows.

Clickety Clark nodded with satisfaction as he watched the brown wreck putter off into the distance. 'Making it easy for us,' he said. 'OK, let's go!'

Blunt gunned the engine, and the Jaguar eased across the road. It slid to a halt across the entrance to Gary's gravel drive. Nobody was going to escape from the cottage that way.

Chapter Twenty-Nine

In the hammock Tammy Jacket was once again asleep. Her even breathing mingled with the hum of insects in the summer idyll. Mrs Pargeter sat at the table and drained the last of her glass of Chardonnay. Definitely deserve another one, she thought. I really think I've finally cracked what's been going on in this case.

Her hand was arrested in midpour by the appearance of two men round the corner of the cottage. The one she hadn't met before was carrying Gary's petrol-driven strimmer, at the end of which the circular metal blade gleamed in the sunlight.

With a steady hand, Mrs Pargeter put the wine bottle down, leaving her glass half-full. 'Good morning, Mr Clark. Oh, sorry, of course you like to be called Clix, don't you?'

The photographer flicked his ponytail back, and grinned ominously. 'Good morning, Mrs Pargeter. Oh, sorry. Hope you don't mind me calling you that, but I think we can dispense with the Lady Entwistle nonsense now, can't we?'

She smiled, giving the impression of a coolness she did not feel, and gestured to the Chardonnay bottle. 'Could I offer you a drink at all?'

'I don't think so, thank you,' said Clickety Clark.

Mrs Pargeter turned the beam of her smile on his companion. 'And what about you? I'm sorry, we haven't actually met, but I do know who you are. I've seen a photograph of you — two photographs of you, actually. Not that I think you were looking your best in either of them.' She was starting to babble now, in the face of the man's implacable stare. 'Still, probably prison photographers aren't the best people to encourage an air of cheerfulness in their sitters. I'm sure you'd get better pictures if you had yourself done by your friend Clix — such a clever photographer, isn't he? Sorry, I am chattering on, aren't I?' She waved again towards the wine bottle. 'Sure I can't tempt you, Mr Blunt?'

By way of answer, his large hand seized the ripcord of the strimmer, and savagely tugged the motor into life. The petrol engine roared; the metal blade whirled. Blunt raised it and advanced towards Mrs Pargeter.

She rose from her chair and edged uneasily around the far side of the table. Blunt made a transverse sweep with the strimmer, scything through the stem of her wineglass.

Holding her hands up to protect her face from the flying shards, Mrs Pargeter backed round the table, away from the hammock, where Tammy still slept in blissful ignorance.

Blunt continued his slow advance, the hissing strimmer held before him like a flame thrower.

At his shoulder, Clickety Clark smiled unpleasantly.

'You've been causing us rather a lot of problems, Mrs Pargeter,' the photographer said. 'You and . . .' he pointed to Tammy Jacket, '. . . *her.*'

Impassively, with strimmer upraised, Blunt moved towards the hammock. It was amazing that Tammy didn't wake as the whirring blade hovered over her face.

'No!' Mrs Pargeter screamed. 'Don't hurt her! Don't —'

With a malicious grin, Blunt suddenly shifted position and brought the spinning metal edge down on the rope that secured the far end of the hammock to a tree. It went through like a knife in spaghetti. The hammock collapsed, spilling a bleary Tammy down with a thud on to the grass.

It didn't take her long to wake up, once she saw the two men looming over her. 'Oh no!' she screamed, scrambling untidily to her feet. She jumped out of the way, as Blunt swung the whirring strimmer in a wide arc at waist height.

Fortunately, the arc was too wide. Missing its target, the blade slammed screaming into the tree from which the hammock had been suspended. With an oath, Blunt moved forward to pull the strimmer free. Clickety Clark followed to help him out.

Mrs Pargeter seized the moment. The two men had their backs to her. Lowering her shoulder, she cannoned the full force of her considerable bulk into Clickety Clark's denim-clad torso. He clattered into Blunt, who was off-balance as he pulled on the strimmer's handle. Both men collapsed in an untidy heap on the floor.

'Quick!' Mrs Pargeter grabbed Tammy Jacket's hand and rushed her down the end of the garden. The only possible means of escape was Gary's little cultivator/tractor. And that only seated one.

'Get in there!' Unceremoniously, Tammy was bundled into the trailer, where she sprawled on a pile of grass and hedge clippings. Then Mrs Pargeter leapt astride the cultivator, and turned the key in the ignition.

The little red engine puttered into life. Mrs Pargeter swung the wheel violently, and the cultivator swerved around, flicking its trailer like a whip-end. Tammy was slammed against the side. For a moment the trailer teetered on one wheel, set to overturn; then the tug of the accelerating cultivator righted it. Tractor and trailer surged through a gap in the hedge to the fields behind.

Having picked himself up, Blunt abandoned the strimmer in favour of more conventional weaponry. The pistol was in his grasp and trained on the two women, when he felt a restraining hand on his arm.

'Not here,' said Clickety Clark. 'Too many explanations.'

Reluctantly, Blunt lowered the gun. His friend tapped him lightly on the shoulder. 'Don't worry. They can't get far. Those fields are bounded by roads. We'll head them off in the car.'

And the two men hurried round the front of

the cottage to their Jaguar.

Mrs Pargeter's white hair streamed in the wind, as the cultivator bounced over the uneven ridges of the sun-baked fields. Tammy Jacket's copper helmet remained rigidly lacquered in place, however violent the bumps and jolts the trailer suffered.

'We'll get through that gate over there!' Mrs Pargeter shouted over her shoulder, the words snatched away by the wind and the sound of the cultivator's motor.

'Probably Tuesday, so long as I can get an appointment!' Tammy Jacket shouted back.

The Jaguar cruised easily along the country road. On either side were fields, cordoned by thick hedgerows. Blunt drove, while Clickety Clark kept his eye on the hedge, through the gaps of which he monitored the approach of the little red cultivator.

'There's nowhere for them to go, you see,' he observed complacently. 'Just got to make for that gate along there. And then we can pick them up at our leisure.'

The Jaguar idled even slower as they crawled towards the gate, which was made of solid tubular metal.

'Good,' said Clickety Clark. 'If it was wood, they might try to smash through. They'll kill themselves if they go into that.'

'Park across it?' asked Blunt. Which was a

long sentence for him.

'No, just to this side,' Clickety Clark replied. 'Then they won't see us, and we can spring them when they stop to open the gate.'

The cultivator's motor screamed protest as Mrs Pargeter flattened the accelerator. The metal gate ahead grew larger at alarming speed, as tractor and trailer hurtled towards it.

'Suppose they're there!' Tammy Jacket shouted into Mrs Pargeter's ear.

'They *are* there! I can see the blue of the Jaguar through the hedge!'

'So what're we going to do!'

'What *you're* going to do,' Mrs Pargeter screamed back, 'is hang on to your hairstyle!'

They were almost upon the gate when she spoke. Clickety Clark and Blunt moved complacently out of hiding to face them over the metal rails.

And just at that moment, Mrs Pargeter suddenly swung the cultivator's steering wheel right. The machine, swirling its trailer like a flamenco dancer's skirt, violently changed course.

'Aagh!' Tammy Jacket squealed. 'We're going straight into the he-e-e-edge!!!'

Her voice was lost as the cultivator smashed through brushwood on to the hard surface of the road behind the parked Jaguar. Mrs Pargeter had a momentary glimpse of the bewildered backward-turned faces of Clickety Clark and Blunt before the cultivator smashed through the next hedge and into the field on the other side.

'Jeromino!' she shouted.

It wasn't something she usually shouted. In fact, it was something she had never shouted before in her entire life.

But it was something she had always wanted to shout.

Chapter Thirty

Geography was against Mrs Pargeter and Tammy Jacket. Though they'd escaped from one field into another, the second one wasn't going to last for ever. It was edged on four sides by roads; beyond the road they were making for there was a river. The cultivator might be able to smash through a hedge; there was no way it could jump over a river. They'd have to stay on the road.

Though the Jaguar couldn't cope with the rough open terrain, roads of course were its element. In a flat race on a tarmac surface, the different engine capabilities of the cultivator and the car would become all too hideously apparent.

Mrs Pargeter swiftly made these calculations, as they passed out of the far side of the field on to the road. Their exit was considerably more decorous than their entrance had been. No pulverized hedgerow this time, no leaves and twigs in their hair. Mrs Pargeter simply stopped the cultivator by a gate, and waited while her trailer passenger opened it.

'Which way do we go?' asked Tammy anxiously, as she climbed back on to her bed of garden refuse.

'Left,' said Mrs Pargeter firmly.

'They're going to catch up with us! There're

no other routes we could have taken. They know where we are!'

'Yes, but we've got a head start on them.' Mrs Pargeter gunned the engine — insofar as the engine of a cultivator/tractor admits of gunning. And what, she wondered idly as she did it, does 'gunning' an engine mean, anyway?

'Have you any idea where we're going?' Tammy Jacket still sounded anxious and a bit whiney.

'Yes,' Mrs Pargeter replied with a confident smile. 'We're going to get help.'

The knot had been tied, the young couple were man and wife, and the reception was going awfully well. The photographs had been efficiently dispatched, and the guests, on arriving at the country house hotel from the church, had been given a glass of champagne *before* all the hand-shaking in the reception line — which is always the sign of a well-organized wedding.

The food had been consumed; everyone had commented on how radiant the bride, how noble the groom, how pretty the little bridesmaids had looked; the photocall for the cutting of the cake had passed without a hitch; and the speeches had been unembarrassing. An elderly uncle's indulgent reminiscences of the eighteen-month-old bride lying naked on a fur rug had prompted appropriate chortles; and the one rather off-colour innuendo in the best man's speech had fortunately not been understood by those whom it might have offended (while those who did understand it had thought it very funny).

All through, champagne flowed exactly as champagne should. The only person not imbibing was Gary, who sat proudly in his uniform on the periphery of the reception, sipping at a glass of fizzy mineral water.

The bride and groom gazed at each other radiantly. It was all going so well. They'd broken the back of it now, the difficult bit was nearly over. Soon they would change into their 'going-away' clothes, be taken by Rolls-Royce to the airport, and finally, mercifully, be on their own. Then the flight to Las Palmas, cab to their hotel, and the wedding night. They had no worries about that last bit; it was the one part of the proceedings they had really practised properly.

The bride glanced at her watch, and the groom took his cue. They'd both been to too many weddings that had gone on too long because the newly-weds had oversocialized rather than doing the decent thing — in other words, going to get changed for departure as soon as possible. So the bride and groom hurried off to the assigned bedroom for a quick change and a quick feel.

They had chosen the right moment. The wedding guests were getting to the stage when they'd soon have to decide whether to start sobering up or to continue and get properly drunk. Long-lost relatives, reunited in the bonhomie of the occasion, were beginning to remember why they'd been long-lost for so long. Tenuous acquaintances, yoked arbitrarily together by the seating plan, were getting to the third cycle of questions about what people did for a living and how many children they had. All good things have to come to an end, and it was time for this particular good thing to come to an end.

In the bedroom upstairs, now dressed in her smart beige 'going-away' suit, the bride looked out over the front drive of the hotel while her new husband brushed his hair at the dressing table. 'It's really beautiful, this. We'll remember it always, won't we?'

'Yes,' agreed her husband, who had shrewdly recognized early in their relationship that that was going to be the best answer to most of her questions.

'Really elegant,' the bride continued, looking down over the neat gravel between perfectly edged lawns on which dark trees were scattered with an eighteenth-century landscape artist's skill. At the centre of the gravel circle directly in front of the hotel stood a fountain round which fat stone cherubs curled, dispensing their cornucopias of water.

'Been a perfect day, hasn't it? Best day of our lives.'

'Yes,' her husband once again concurred, knowing which side his bread was buttered.

Downstairs, Gary and Denise discreetly left the ballroom in which the reception was being held. He wanted to check that all was ready for a trouble-free departure in the Rolls-Royce.

'Oh, for God's sake!' he said, as he came out of the hotel's front doors. 'Haven't they got any respect for a classic?'

Some waggish friends of the groom had been at work. Across the Rolls-Royce's back window the words 'Just Married' had been picked out in shaving foam. The rear bumper had been wrapped in pink toilet roll, and a cluster of tin cans tied on to jangle against the road.

Gary moved forward, reaching instinctively into his pocket for a handkerchief to wipe off the foam.

'No, you don't,' said Denise.

'But it's my Rolls-Royce,' Gary protested pathetically.

'You don't,' his wife continued, 'a, because that's what people pay for when they hire wedding cars, and b, because you certainly don't wipe it off with your clean handkerchief. Is that clear?'

'Yes,' replied Gary, who had long since learned the same lesson as the bridegroom in the bedroom above. 'So what do I do?'

'You make no comment at all. You drive them to the airport with the tin cans clanking behind — and you just hope nobody's stuffed a kipper up the exhaust . . .'

'Oh, no!' Gary rushed round the back of the car and crouched to check whether his precious Rolls-Royce had suffered this final indignity. He sighed with relief. There was no smell or other evidence of fishy sabotage.

'And,' Denise continued when he rose to his

feet, 'next time you take a wedding booking — particularly when it involves the Roller — you make sure you charge a lot more.'

'Right.'

'You got to cover the depreciation of your motors.'

'True.'

'So you put on a "foam, toilet roll and tin can surcharge" — right?'

'Right.'

Denise turned at the sound of the hotel front doors opening. 'Oh, they're coming. I'll get a lift back — see you at home, love.'

'Yes, OK.' Averting his eyes from the desecration of his precious Rolls-Royce, the uniformed chauffeur got into the driving seat and adjusted the line of his cap in the rear-view mirror.

Denise melted back to join the emerging wedding party. The bride and groom, pale-suited and casual, stood out against the crowd of morning dress and hats. Hands were slapped on shoulders, jocular platitudes about honeymoons were tossed into the mêlée. The bride's mother wondered whether it was her cue to have a little cry or not.

At that moment, communal attention was snatched away from the happy couple by an apparition at the end of the hotel's drive. Through the impressive iron gates, its engine screaming resistance to the way it was being driven, surged, in a spray of gravel, a small red cultivator/tractor with a trailer of garden debris in tow.

The tractor was being driven by a white-haired

woman in a bright silk dress. Bouncing about in the trailer behind was a copper-headed woman dressed in an unlikely miscellany of clashing garments. The pair of them were screeching up the drive at a terrifying rate.

Even more alarming, behind them, eating up the space between the two vehicles, surged a huge blue Jaguar. The two grim faces behind its windscreen were oblivious to their surroundings, obsessed only by the imperative of the chase.

The wedding party watched open-mouthed as the cultivator skidded to an untidy halt beside the fountain. The two women leapt off and rushed towards the white-ribboned Rolls-Royce. The older one opened the back door, bustled the younger inside, and leapt in after her.

The Rolls-Royce immediately burst into life, reversing, in a clatter of tin cans, away from the approaching Jaguar. The Jaguar suddenly swung right, away from the fountain, turning in a wide arc, searing through the carpet of lawns to head off the Roller if it tried to escape down the drive.

But the Rolls-Royce's driver knew his stuff. Suddenly spinning his steering wheel, he shot across the gravel between the abandoned cultivator and the fountain.

The Jaguar, its driver realizing their quarry wasn't making for the main gates, continued in the turning circle on which it was set, homing back towards the hotel, targeted to hit the Rolls-Royce broadsides.

The mouths of the wedding guests gaped further, and they tensed themselves for the impact.

Just at the second the smash seemed inevitable, the Rolls-Royce shot forward. Skating over the gravel on two wheels, it spun at a crazy angle before righting itself on the grass. Scoring deep furrows across the green, it sped towards the hotel gates.

The Jaguar had not had time to change course. It smashed heavily into the fountain. A stone cherub, surprised by the impact, fell on to the bonnet, bounced and smashed through the windscreen.

A second cherub, less completely dislodged, leant away from the fountain at a crazy angle. From the cornucopia held in its hands, water poured through the broken glass on to the heads of the two dazed men.

The hotel manager, drawn by the noise, came out to witness the devastation of his fountain and the ravaging of his lawns.

His jaw dropped even further than those of the wedding guests. Particularly when he caught sight of a Rolls-Royce, which trailed a cacophony of tin cans and had 'Just Married' sprayed in foam across its back window, disappearing at high speed out of his hotel gates.

A scream of complaining metal drew attention back to the Jaguar. It screeched backwards, spraying gravel like a nail-bomb, howled back into forward gear, and hurtled off across the lawns in pursuit of the Rolls-Royce.

The bride turned to the bridegroom, and burst into tears. 'This is the worst day of my life!' she wailed. 'Isn't it?'

'Yes,' said the bridegroom, playing safe.

Chapter Thirty-One

The Rolls-Royce was a powerful beast, but it wasn't built for speed to the same extent as the Jaguar. Blunt and Clickety Clark's collision with the fountain had made a hell of a mess of the car's bodywork, but didn't seem to have affected the engine. As the two vehicles hurtled through country lanes, the gap between them narrowed inexorably.

'Where're you making for, Gary?' Mrs Pargeter shouted from the back seat.

'Back to my place!'

'Why? Have you got staff there who can help us?'

'No,' Gary replied grimly. 'I got shooters.'

'Shooters? But I thought you didn't approve of —'

'I don't as a rule. But then, as a rule, I'm not up against Blunt. No way he won't have a gun on him.'

'He has!' Tammy Jacket wailed. 'I seen it! He was about to take a potshot at us when we escaped on the tractor.'

'I knew it. I've got an old sawn-off back of my barn. That'll even up the odds a bit.'

Mrs Pargeter pursed her lips. 'You know I don't approve of guns unless they're absolutely unavoidable.'

'They're unavoidable this time. I don't fancy facing up to Blunt with only the natural charm of my personality to protect me.'

'My late husband always said,' Mrs Pargeter continued primly, 'that those who live by the gun are extremely likely to die by the gun.'

'Seems reasonable to me,' the chauffeur shouted back. 'Blunt's lived by the gun all right, so he'll only be getting his due.'

'Well, Gary, if there's any way of avoiding violence . . .'

'Sure, sure, Mrs P. I'll do me best. Hold on tight, we're nearly there!'

The cottage loomed ahead like a jet-propelled chocolate box. The Jaguar was now so close behind the Rolls-Royce that Mrs Pargeter could almost count Blunt's nasal hairs, when Gary suddenly swung the steering wheel right into his drive. He spun into the opposite lock, heading straight for the barn garage. Both sets of doors were open, so that the structure appeared like a bridge.

Just as they were steaming into the building, Gary caught sight of the banner flapping over the doorway. 'What the hell . . .' he mouthed in disbelief.

Mrs Pargeter looked up, and managed to read the words blazoned across the white sheet before the car swept into the barn. With a sense of doom, she recognized the logo, and the inevitable legend:

WHAT'S THE FIRST THING TO DO WHEN YOU
GET YOUR OWN FLAT?
RE-TIRE.

She just had time to register that Fossilface
O'Donahue's understanding of joke structure was
still improving, when her attention was seized by
a shriek of 'Good heavens, look at that lot!' from
Gary.

In the microsecond that they were inside the
barn, she saw the high-heaped towers that filled
the entire structure except for the narrow channel
through which the Rolls-Royce sped. And she
recognized that the huge piles were built up of
brand-new car tyres. Fossilface O'Donahue was
once again paying his dues, once again in what
he thought was an appropriate fashion. In the past
he'd once sabotaged one of Gary's tyres; now the
chauffeur had more tyres than he could ever possibly need. Oh yes, another triumph for the cock-
eyed logic of Fossilface O'Donahue.

Gary slammed the brakes on the minute his
Roller was in the maintenance yard, and reached
for his door handle. 'I'll get the sawn-off and deal
with the . . .'

His words trickled away at the sights and
sounds emerging from the barn. The Jaguar, only
metres behind them, had swung savagely into the
narrow passageway.

Too savagely. A bumper had caught the base
of one of the tyre towers, setting the whole edifice
wobbling. That tower destabilized the others. A

few random tyres toppled down, then little flurries of them fell; finally, in an avalanche of rubber, all the tyres in the barn collapsed inwards, burying the immobilized Jaguar under their combined weight.

'You know,' Mrs Pargeter observed, 'I think, for the first time, one of Fossilface's acts of "restitooshun" has actually done someone some good.'

Chapter Thirty-Two

Even with its shaving-foam inscription and wake of tin cans and toilet rolls, Gary's Rolls-Royce still contrived to appear majestic as it processed over Vauxhall Bridge. The two ladies in the back were looking somewhat better than they had when leaving their former transport at the country house hotel. Gary's new Roller was stocked for every eventuality. There was a supply of cosmetics and toiletries in the back pocket, and the two passengers had used these to repair their make-up and hair-styles (though in Tammy Jacket's case, not a single hair of her lacquered helmet had shifted).

Amongst its other supplies, the Rolls-Royce also had a well-stocked drinks cabinet and Mrs Pargeter, once her appearance was restored to elegance, had immediately started pouring. As she concluded her call on the carphone, she was on her third vodka Campari, while Tammy Jacket kept pace with her in brandy and ginger ale.

'It's all right, Truffler. We're fine.'

'I still should've thought. Should've kept my eyes skinned for those two villains when I was leaving Gary's place.' His voice, from the other end of the phone, was heavy with self-recrimination.

'You had no means of knowing they were on to me. It was my own fault for thinking I could get away with the Lady Entwistle disguise. You warned me not to try that on, Truffler, but I just wouldn't listen, would I?'

'No . . .' he agreed, slightly cheered by her redistribution of blame. 'Look, is there anything else you need me to do — apart from what we've talked about?'

Mrs Pargeter was thoughtful for a moment before she replied, 'No, no, there's something else I need doing, but . . . sewing up the case against Blunt and Clickety Clark is more urgent. You get on with that.'

'OK. What was the other thing needs doing? You might as well tell me.'

'Just I think I ought to have another word with Fossilface O'Donahue. Job he done on Gary turned out for the good, as it happened, but that was pure chance. Fossilface is still a bit of a loose cannon out there. I think I ought to try to stop his programme of "restitooshun".'

'Well, it's soon going to come to a natural end, innit? Not many people left he needs to pay back, are there?'

'No, I suppose not. Still feel I should have a word with him, though. Who *does* he still need to make "restitooshun" to, as a matter of interest?'

'Well, he's done you . . . me — blast his eyes! . . . Keyhole Crabbe . . . Hedgeclipper . . . now Gary . . . I guess there's only Concrete Jacket left, of the ones I know about. And he can't touch

Concrete while he's in the nick, can he?'

'He touched Keyhole while *he* was in the nick, didn't he?'

'Hm. You may have a point.'

'Truffler, tell me . . . in what way did Fossilface do the dirty on Concrete? Just so's we know what we may be up against.'

'Worse thing he ever done to Concrete was . . . he didn't call the police.'

'What do you mean?'

'Concrete was working on this complicated job. It was an art theft. Couple of paintings from a gallery in Cork Street. One was a Rembrandt, I seem to remember. Concrete'd got it worked out. Soon as he broke in, the gallery's alarm'd sound in the local nick. Boys in blue'd set off to get him, but just when they're near, Fossilface O'Donahue, who's got this radio set that cuts in on their frequency, is meant to ring through, say it was a false alarm, and could they go off to deal with an environmentalists' riot outside the Brazilian Embassy? Would've worked a treat . . . only Fossilface never made the call.'

'Ah.'

'Concrete was away from his missus four years after that.'

'Oh dear.'

'Mind you, what kind of "restitooshun" Fossilface O'Donahue would plan for that . . . I just cannot begin to imagine.'

'No. Anyway, don't you worry about that, Truffler. You just concentrate on what we discussed. I'll have a go at contacting Fossilface. Talk soon — OK? Bye.'

She returned the handset to its cradle, and took a long sip from her drink.

Truffler getting on all right then, is he?' called Gary from the front.

'He's fine. Just sorting out the loose ends of the case. Checking whether there was anyone else involved apart from Clickety Clark and Blunt.' With a triumphant grin, Mrs Pargeter turned to Tammy. 'Truffler's going to build up a nice little dossier — all the details, all the evidence — which is guaranteed to get those two villains put away for a very long time . . .' She took the other woman's hand, and gave it a reassuring squeeze. 'And then we'll get Concrete off the hook.'

Tammy Jacket smiled her wordless gratitude.

No one would have suspected that the elegant white-haired lady who stepped out of a Rolls-Royce in a street near Victoria Station had, only an hour and a half earlier, been driving a cultivator/tractor through a series of hedges. She looked exactly like someone whose sole business of the day had been a visit to a solicitor. She looked as decorous and correct as the shining brass plate on the door outside which the Rolls-Royce had parked. The plate read: Nigel Merriman — Solicitor and Commissioner for Oaths.

'Sure you don't want me to hang around?' asked Gary, as he closed the car door behind her.

'No, you go and see if Truffler needs any help.'

Mrs Pargeter leant through the open back window to kiss Tammy Jacket tenderly on the cheek. 'You'll be fine, love. Take care now.' Then she turned back to Gary. 'And one of your drivers will get Tammy home safely?'

The woman in the back of the car looked at her with some alarm. 'It's all right, I promise,' Mrs Pargeter reassured her. 'Those two won't come troubling you again.'

'It's not just that,' said Tammy. 'It's the thought of going back to all the horrible mess, and seeing all my lovely things smashed and —'

'No worries.' Mrs Pargeter laid a hand on her arm. 'I've had the place tidied up for you. Looks just like new — well, nearly.'

'Oh, Mrs Pargeter . . .' was all that Tammy Jacket could say. She was almost weeping with gratitude.

'Who you get to do the clean-up?' asked Gary, in a whisper.

'Guy called Meredith the Mop. Found his name in my late husband's address book. Apparently he's very good at tidying up after things.'

'I'll say! He did that mop-up operation after the Crouch End Pizza House incident. Lovely job he done. Got all the burn-marks off the bar counter, filled in the bullet-holes in the walls, and nobody could imagine how he managed to get all the blood out of the table cloths. I tell you, it was —'

The chauffeur caught the expression in the violet-blue eyes that were trained on his, and decided that he'd probably said enough.

'Gary,' Mrs Pargeter intoned glacially, 'I have no idea what on earth you're talking about.' Then she leant once again in through the car window. 'Chin up, Tammy. You just go home and wait for Concrete. Won't be long now till he's home, I promise you that.'

Chapter Thirty-Three

Mrs Pargeter's eyes sparkled as she rounded off her exposition of the case. There was something very satisfying about having all the details sorted out, all the loose ends neatly tied up. Opposite her sat Nigel Merriman, formal and impassive, giving no reaction to her revelations, but occasionally scribbling a note on the legal pad in front of him.

At the conclusion of her narrative, he asked, 'And you say Mr Mason'll be able to prove all this?'

She grinned confidently. 'Oh yes, Truffler's sorting out the evidence even as we speak. And he's good at that sort of stuff. It'll be rock solid, don't you worry.'

'Hm. And you're sure it was just the two of them . . .' he looked down at his pad, and fastidiously pronounced the unfamiliar names, '. . . Clickety Clark and Blunt . . . who organized the whole thing? You don't think that someone else may have been organizing *them?*'

'I don't think there was anyone else, but Truffler's checking that out, too. Don't worry, Nigel. There's easily enough to get Concrete Jacket off now, isn't there?'

Nigel Merriman's face took on the expression

of professional caution that goes with the job, but he couldn't help agreeing. 'Oh, certainly. I don't see how the authorities could possibly keep hold of my client if all this were to be made public. No, you've done extremely well, Mrs Pargeter.'

'Thank you,' she said modestly.

There was a knock at the door behind her. 'Come in,' said the solicitor automatically and then continued addressing Mrs Pargeter. 'You seem to have sorted out the whole thing with admirable efficiency. In fact, there's really only one detail in the case you got wrong.'

'And what was that?' asked Mrs Pargeter combatively. She felt pretty certain she'd made sense of the whole scenario, and was confidently prepared to argue her case.

She heard the door behind her open, and saw Nigel Merriman's eyeline move to his new visitors. His expression had changed. Now it contained something gleeful. Unpleasantly gleeful.

With sickening certainty of what she was about to see, Mrs Pargeter slowly turned round.

Framed in the doorway, their faces bruised and scarred, and looking meaner than she'd ever seen them look before, were Clickety Clark and Blunt.

Chapter Thirty-Four

There was no give in the rope that tied Mrs Pargeter's arms behind the chair and her legs to the chair legs. Her captors had made it clear that the smallest sound from her would result in her mouth being taped over with equal tightness. The outer door of the office had been firmly locked by a large key So she could only watch helplessly what was going on.

The thick curtains had been drawn, presumably to avoid anything being seen from adjacent blocks, and the lights were on. The surface of Nigel Merriman's desk was covered with wads of banknotes, which Clickety Clark and Blunt were transferring systematically into a series of brief-cases.

While they did this, the solicitor watched them, swivelling idly in his chair and playing with the point of a paperknife. He seemed much more relaxed now. His professional formality had been replaced by an impudent, almost daredevil, cheerfulness, as he spelled out the revised situation to his captive.

'The only effect your meddling will have had on us, Mrs Pargeter, is to move our plans forward a little. We had intended to leave the country at the end of the year, but we've got the bulk of the money together, so . . .' he shrugged carelessly, '. . . to make our departure now will represent no problem.'

As she had before in similar situations, Mrs Pargeter tried the breezy, facetious approach. 'Oh well, if I haven't caused you any problem, then you can just set me free, can't you?' she suggested.

Her flippancy raised a thin smile from Nigel Merriman, but that was the full extent of its reward. 'Ah, Mrs Pargeter . . . if only life were that simple. You see, you do know rather a lot about us. In fact, I was impressed by how much you managed to work out . . . and of course I was grateful for the way you kept telling me all about it. But . . . I'm afraid you do know a little too much to be allowed back into circulation.'

As he spoke, he reached into his desk drawer, and pulled out a stubby but businesslike automatic pistol. He gave a helpless shrug, as if he were at the mercy of forces beyond his control. 'Sorry about this, Mrs Pargeter. Still, I suppose, in a way, it'll be a kind of double for me.'

'What do you mean?'

He gave her a bland smile, as he rose from his seat and began to move expansively around the office. 'Now — getting my own back on you. And before that — getting my own back on your husband . . .'

Suddenly Mrs Pargeter understood. Her late husband's professional life had been conducted in a general atmosphere of goodwill and mutual cooperation, marred only by the occasional minor unpleasantness.

And one major unpleasantness. The occasion when the late Mr Pargeter's natural bonhomie and trusting nature had been betrayed by one of his most trusted associates. The occasion when this evil man — Julian Embridge — had suborned others of the late Mr Pargeter's entourage, men who had benefited hugely from their employer's instinctive philanthropy, and persuaded them to join him in his perfidy. The ghastly incident had been known thereafter simply by the name of the place where it had been perpetrated. The name unfailingly sent a chill through Mrs Pargeter's heart, and she felt that familiar uneasy *frisson* as she murmured, 'Streatham?'

Nigel Merriman stopped his circuit of the room and nodded smugly. He was now standing between his quarry and the outer door. 'Yes, I was one of the people involved in events in Streatham, Mrs Pargeter. Though — perhaps luckily for me — your husband was never made aware of my participation.'

He was impervious to the look of undiluted hatred that she trained on him. Nor was he aware of the tiny change that came into her expression as she noticed a slight movement behind him. Mrs Pargeter looked firmly into the solicitor's eyes to absorb his concentration, but still her peripheral vision watched in fascination what was happening to the outer door.

A tiny hand, at the end of a tiny fur-covered

arm, was reaching in through the door's letter-box. Slowly, the hand snaked towards the large key in the lock.

'You won't get away with killing me, Nigel,' said Mrs Pargeter, desperate to monopolize his attention. 'I've got a lot of friends — a lot of my late husband's former colleagues — who'll come after you and find you.'

The solicitor let out a little dry laugh. 'I don't think they'll find me where I'm going, Mrs Pargeter. We've got the perfect bolt-hole, don't you worry. This whole thing has been worked out in rather a lot of detail — and I'm particularly good on detail. One of the benefits of my legal training.'

Out of the corner of her eye, Mrs Pargeter saw the tiny fingers extract the key from its lock, and saw the hand slowly withdraw. As the metal scraped against the frame of the letter-box, she was terrified that Nigel Merriman would hear, but he was far too jubilantly caught up in his triumph to notice anything else.

'No, I'm sorry,' he continued. 'You just represent too much of a risk for us to contemplate your getting out of this alive.' He raised the automatic pistol till the end of its barrel was only millimetres away from her temple.

'So now,' he said, his voice laden down with mock regret, 'I'm afraid, Mrs Pargeter, the time has come to —'

The lights in the room were suddenly out. Mrs Pargeter felt herself falling as her chair was knocked violently sideways. There was a confusion of thumps, shouts, a gunshot and, above everything, the gleeful chattering of a triumphant marmoset.

Chapter Thirty-Five

The tables had been very effectively turned. The restraining ropes now attached Clickety Clark, Blunt and Nigel Merriman to office chairs. And since the three of them had proved unwilling to maintain a voluntary silence, the decision had been taken to affix firm strips of plaster across their mouths.

Mrs Pargeter beamed with satisfaction at the handiwork of her saviours. Truffler Mason, Gary and Hedgeclipper Clinton looked becomingly modest, but there was an undeniable air of satisfaction about their demeanour too. Erasmus was more overt in his triumphalism. He seemed to understand the importance of his contribution to the rescue, and circled the office in a continuing lap of honour, chattering self-congratulation, as he leapt from desks, chairs, and the heads of the three trussed malefactors.

Truffler surveyed the scene with that gaze of desolation which those who knew him well recognized as euphoria. 'You know, Mrs Pargeter, it has to be said that your late husband did teach us how to do certain things extraordinarily well.'

'Yes. Yes, he did,' she agreed, perhaps for a moment a mite tearful. But she shook herself briskly out of sentimentality. 'I still can't believe my good fortune that you lot arrived when you did.'

'Wasn't good fortune,' said Truffler. 'It was research. I said I'd find out whether Clickety Clark and Blunt were acting on their own or whether they weren't. And I found out they weren't.' He looked across at Nigel Merriman with unqualified distaste. 'And I found out who their puppet-master was. *And* I found out that he'd been involved in Streatham.'

Mrs Pargeter calmed the rising belligerence in his tone. 'No personal revenge, Truffler. As usual, we'll go through the official channels . . .'

There was a sound — not so definite as a groan, more a sigh — of dissent and disappointment from her three rescuers.

'. . . like the law-abiding citizens we are,' Mrs Pargeter concluded firmly. Then a sheepish expression came into her face. 'Mind you, I am rather ashamed that I had to be rescued by a monkey.'

'Particularly after all the nasty things you said about Erasmus.' Hedgeclipper Clinton's tone was reproving. The marmoset, apparently reacting to the mention of his name, jumped from the top of Nigel Merriman's head on to his owner's shoulder, and sat there looking pious and self-righteous. 'I haven't actually heard you say a proper thank-you to him yet, Mrs Pargeter,' Hedgeclipper prompted.

She looked balefully at the monkey. It returned an unflinching stare. The two of them were never going to like each other, but maybe some kind of mutual respect might in time evolve. 'Thank you very much, Erasmus,' Mrs Pargeter mumbled. Then, relieved to have got that unpalatable task out of the way, she moved swiftly on. 'All right, Truffler, let's get to work.'

'Certainly.' His resentment of a few moments before instantly forgotten, the detective moved across the office and coiled his long body into a chair facing a word processor, which he switched on. 'OK. Ready to go.'

'We need all the evidence spelled out in minute detail.'

'Don't worry, Mrs P. I'm used to doing that. What distinguishes a good detective from an in-different one is the kind of report he writes and, though I say it myself, I do write a bloody good report. Going to take some time, though.'

'We can wait.' Mrs Pargeter looked around the room. 'Be nicer if we had a drink while we sit waiting, though, wouldn't it?' She looked across at Nigel Merriman, whose dull eyes glared loath-ing over his plaster-covered mouth. 'Too much to hope that you'd have a nice little drinks fridge for your clients, eh, Nigel? Far too tight-fisted, I imagine.'

Something in the solicitor's body language con-firmed that her guess had been correct. 'Oh well, never mind.'

'Mrs Pargeter, allow me,' said Hedgeclipper Clinton, his hotelier manner at its most unctuous. In his managerial black jacket and pinstripes, he looked entirely at home in a solicitor's office. The image, as ever, was only let down by the marmoset on his shoulder.

He reached a telephone from the desk and punched in a number. 'Ah, Mario, could you do me a special delivery? Yes, sort of room service, though the room in question is not actually in the hotel.' He gave Nigel Merriman's address. 'Three bottles of the Dom Perignon . . . The '48, yes. Very cold. Four of the crystal goblets . . .'

His eyebrows responded to Gary's upraised hand. 'Hm?'

'Could we have some mineral water, and all? 'Cause I'm driving.'

'Of course. Still or sparkling?'

'Sparkling, please.'

'Mario,' Hedgeclipper continued into the receiver, 'could we add a bottle of sparkling mineral water . . . Oh, and some of those more-money-than-sense-customer wedding snacks . . . Yes, you know, the Japanese titbits . . . Smoked salmon, obviously . . . The quails' eggs, and the caviar, yes — red and black . . . I think that's probably it . . .' A frenetic screeching from his shoulder made him aware of an omission. 'Oh, and an extremely large bunch of bananas. Soon as possible, Mario, thank you.'

He put the phone down and beamed across at Mrs Pargeter. 'Be about ten minutes. Then we'll have a little something to sip and nibble while we wait for Truffler to complete his *magnum opus*.'

There was a contented silence in the office,

interrupted only by the plastic clacking of Truffler Mason's fingers on the keyboard, and the scratching of Erasmus's claws as he explored Clickety Clark's thinning hair for nits.

'Presumably, once it's all written up, you'll hand it over to the filth — er, the police authorities?' asked Hedgeclipper Clinton.

Mrs Pargeter nodded. 'That's right. Direct them here.' She gestured to Nigel Merriman's desk, on which the piles of banknotes and the half-filled briefcases lay exactly where they had when the lights went out. 'I think that lot'll probably help to convince them too.'

'Imagine so,' said Gary with a grin. 'I haven't seen that much loot since the famous occasion in that Ponders End depository when Mr Pargeter got the . . .' He caught a look from Mrs Pargeter and seemed suddenly to lose his thread. He began studiously buffing the badge on his peaked cap.

'So spell it all out, Truffler,' she continued serenely, as if the recent moment of potential unpleasantness had never happened.

'Will do.'

'We don't want any room for ambiguity.'

'Don't worry,' said the detective without pausing in his task. 'I'll do it so's a ten-year-old child could understand it.'

Mrs Pargeter looked dubious. 'Truffler, could you make that a five-year-old child? We are dealing with the police here, after all.'

Truffler Mason nodded and continued typing.

Chapter Thirty-Six

The Rolls-Royce, once again gleaming and free of its wedding encumbrances, was parked on a double yellow line directly outside Bow Street Police Station. Gary drummed his fingers on the steering wheel. Hedgeclipper Clinton sat tensely forward in the back seat. Even Erasmus seemed subdued. Only Mrs Pargeter was serenely relaxed, leaning back against the car's luxurious upholstery with a vodka Campari in her hand.

'He's been in there a long time,' Gary murmured after a silence. 'You don't think they've nicked him, do you?'

'What on earth could they nick him for?' asked Mrs Pargeter reasonably. 'Truffler's got no form, no previous convictions, and what he's doing at the moment is certainly not illegal. It's the act of a public-spirited, law-abiding citizen. The police should fall over themselves to welcome people like that. Save them a lot of effort if every member of the public started doing their job for them.'

'Hm.' Gary didn't look entirely convinced. 'I don't know. I still don't like it. Going voluntarily into a police station . . . well, doesn't feel natural. Looks to me like asking for trouble.'

'That attitude,' said Mrs Pargeter with some asperity, 'is a hangover from your past, young

Gary. And it's something you should very definitely have grown out of by now.'

'Yes, all right,' he mumbled truculently.

'Truffler's too canny to say the wrong thing, anyway. Isn't he?' said Hedgeclipper Clinton, without complete conviction.

'Of course he is. Honestly, what's got into you two? You're behaving like a pair of teenage girls at their first dance. Truffler had to see to it personally that the dossier got into the hands of the right person, and that's what he's doing. There won't be any problem.'

At that moment a familiar tall figure emerged from the doors of the police station and walked in a leisurely fashion towards the Rolls-Royce.

'See?' said Mrs Pargeter.

Gary started the engine as Truffler settled into the back seat between Hedgeclipper Clinton and his employer. 'They took it all right?' she asked.

'No problem,' Truffler replied.

'And you're sure they'll act on it straight away?'

'Oh yes. They're raring to go. I should think a squad car's arriving at Nigel Merriman's office even as we speak.'

He sounded so confident, Mrs Pargeter couldn't help asking, 'What did you say?'

Truffler gave a wolfish grin. 'I told them it was three certain arrests, couple of percentage points up on the local clear-up rate, and a good chance of an OBE for the officer in charge.'

'Lovely, Truffler.'

'But they can't've just let you walk out. Didn't

they demand you give them a contact number?' asked Hedgeclipper Clinton, still uneasy.

' 'Course they did.'

'So did you give them one?'

' 'Course I did.'

Mrs Pargeter smiled in pleasant anticipation. 'And who will they get through to if they ring it, Truffler?'

'London Zoo, Mrs P. Then they can have a chat with some of Erasmus's relatives, can't they?'

Mrs Pargeter chuckled as the Rolls-Royce drove off into the night.

Chapter Thirty-Seven

The following day, Truffler Mason had a piece of good news. The manager of the betting shop beneath his office told him that a lot of papers had been found stuffed into a skip in their back yard. On inspection, these turned out to be all the detective's tatty old records, complete to the last scribbled bus ticket.

Truffler was ecstatic. True, some of the precious dust on his papers had been dislodged in their removal, but he felt confident that that would be replaced in time. Even after such a few days, the gleam had already gone from his new office furniture, and the surfaces were beginning to get comfortably cluttered with shreds of paper, newspaper clippings and encrusted coffee cups.

Truffler decided, however, that he would not entirely reject Fossilface O'Donahue's misplaced generosity. Though the detective himself would never change his old methods of finding information, after the scare of believing he'd lost the lot he could recognize the value of having his irreplaceable archive backed up on computer.

To that end he dispatched Bronwen off on a month's computer course. As a matter of fact, his motives for doing this were not unmixed. While he certainly did want to get his archive computerized, he could also see the advantages of having his secretary out of the office until she'd calmed down a little after the courtroom encounter with her latest ex-husband.

In fact, as things turned out, Truffler didn't gain much from his actions. On the course Bronwen met another man who, by the time she came back to the office, was clearly lining up to be her next husband.

Truffler Mason resigned himself to the prospect of history repeating itself again . . . and again . . . and again . . .

At Mrs Pargeter's plot, it was as if nothing had changed. True, Willie Cass's body was no longer lying at the bottom of the embryo wine cellar, nor was there any vestige left on the site of the police investigations. All their tapes and canvas screens, cars and caravans, had gone. The foundations of the house once again marked out their bald relief map, rendered rather desolate by the thin rain that fell unremittingly.

But the weather couldn't dampen Mrs Pargeter's spirits. Now she was back standing on her plot, all the excitement of what was going to happen there once again caught hold of her. Her high heels picked their way almost skittishly through the mud and caked cement dust.

She turned triumphantly to Concrete Jacket, whose gumboots moved along more sedately behind her. 'It's going to be great, isn't it?'

'Certainly is, Mrs P.'

'And everything all right over at your place?'

'You bet.'

'Tammy got her home back just like she wants it?'

'Even better.' He grinned. 'Thing is, all that destruction they done was kind of a blessing in disguise. Give me the opportunity to do the place over, even better. Whole new lot of features I've put in.'

With great control, Mrs Pargeter managed to stop herself from wincing at the thought of what new decorative extravagances Concrete might have perpetrated.

'Glad to hear it. So . . .' she continued, tactfully casual, '. . . with those three villains inside and you cleared of everything, freed without a stain on your character, and your own house all sorted out to Tammy's satisfaction . . . there's nothing to stop you getting on here now, is there, Concrete?'

He grinned magnanimously. 'Not a thing, Mrs Pargeter. Have you settled into the house by Christmas, no problem.'

They were now once again standing by what would in time be the wine cellar. It was loosely boarded over, as it had been on their previous visit. Mrs Pargeter looked down and grinned wryly. 'Hope we haven't got any more nasty surprises in there, Concrete.'

'Don't you worry about a thing,' he said jovially, and moved forward to push the boards aside.

His jaw dropped. 'What the . . .'

They both looked down in amazement. Leaning against the side of the brick-lined well were two paintings. Their age and subject matter suggested they were Old Masters; indeed, the dark browns of the smaller had about them the definite look of a Rembrandt.

Attached to the frame of the larger painting was a sheet of paper. It was headed, Mrs Pargeter observed with a sinking feeling, by a smiley face.

I SAY, I SAY, I SAY, the legend read, WHY DID THEY HANG THAT PICTURE?

I DON'T KNOW, WHY DID THEY HANG THAT PICTURE?

BECAUSE THEY COULDN'T FIND THE ART-IST.

Underneath this a note had been scribbled: 'Don't worry, Concrete. I won't let you down again. This time I've remembered to ring the police.'

'Oh no,' Mrs Pargeter moaned. 'I don't believe . . .'

But her words trailed away in an awful moment of *déjà vu* — or perhaps *déjà entendu*. There was a sound of approaching sirens. Mrs Pargeter and Concrete Jacket turned, and the *déjà entendu* was supplemented by *déjà vu*. They looked down the hill to where two police cars were screeching to a halt beside Gary's Rolls-Royce and the Range Rover.

Mrs Pargeter saw the prospects for her house's completion fade once again away into the distance.

'Oh, *Fossilface!*' she groaned in exasperation.